DON'T YOU KNOW THERE'S A WAR ON?

DON'T YOU KNOW THERE'S A WAR ON?

AVI

SCHOLASTIC INC.

New York Toronto London Auckland Sydney
Mexico City New Delhi Hong Kong Buenos Aires

Dates throughout are the dates that headlines appeared in
newspapers, not the dates that events occurred.

The author gratefully acknowledges John Dunning's
On the Air: The Encyclopedia of Old-Time Radio
(New York: Oxford University Press, 1998)
as the source of quotes on pages 63–64 and 114.

ISBN 0-439-52196-3

12 11 10 9 8 7 6 5 4 3 2   3 4 5 6 7 8/0

Printed in the U.S.A.   40

First Scholastic printing, January 2003

Typography by Hilary Zarycky

For Gail Hochman, of Brooklyn

PART ONE

German Tanks and Guns Battle
Eighth Army Units in North Africa.
U.S. Forces Suffer a Sharp Setback.

German Radio Claims That U-boats
Sank 204,000 Tons of Shipping in a
Convoy Battle.

1943 Draft to Call 12,000 Men Daily
As President Warns Nation It
Faces Reverses in War.

Meatless Days in Restaurants.

1

I WAS LATE that Monday morning because my shoelace broke just as I was leaving for school. Meant I had to use some string. Now, you might think string would be easy to find, but it wasn't. String was something you gave away for the war effort. Besides, my sister had already left for school and my mother was at her job at the Navy Yard. Those days me and my family lived in Brooklyn. During the war. When I was eleven.

Like I was saying, I was supposed to be going to school. Class Five-B, Public School Number Eight. P.S. 8, we called it. The school's real name was The Robert Fulton School, but I never heard no kid call it that.

Anyway, by the time I finally got going down Hicks Street, I was so late no kids were there. Just grown-ups wearing big coats and dark hats. Me? I was dressed in my regular school outfit: bomber jacket, brown corduroy pants, plaid flannel shirt, and a snap-on glossy red necktie that almost reached my middle. Hanging round my neck was what we called a dog tag. Sort of this tin disk with your name and address stamped on it. All us kids had to wear them. You know, in case the enemy attacked like at Pearl Harbor and people wanted to know who your body was.

The name on my tag was Howard Bellington Crispers. But the thing was, the only person who ever used my full name was my mom. And see, she only did when she was mad at me. So mostly people called me Howie. Which worried me, because it wasn't on my tag. I mean, how were they going to identify me if my name wasn't right? By my looks?

Back then I wasn't very tall. But my ears were big, plus I had the same old blue eyes and carrot-colored hair. Though Mom was always making me brush that hair down, it never stood flat. And no matter how much I was in front of the bathroom mirror pressing my ears back, they didn't stay flat neither. These days, being sixteen, I'm taller, but to tell the truth, the hair and the ears, they haven't changed much.

The other thing, that morning it felt like it was going to rain. Which meant my shoes—with the string lace—might get wet. Not so jazzy because, like everybody, we had ration coupons for only three pairs of shoes a year. For the whole family. The point being, you did what you had to do because in those days, no matter what happened, you could always say, "Hey, don't you know there's a war on?" See, it explained anything.

So anyway, there I was, going down Hicks Street carrying my pop's beat-up wooden lunch box. Inside was a peanut butter and jelly sandwich on white Tip Top bread wrapped in paper, plus a graham-cracker snack and this dinky bottle of Borden's chocolate milk. My left hand was holding a canvas satchel with my schoolbooks.

This Hicks Street was narrow, squeezed tight by three-story brownstone houses with stoops. The neighborhood also had some old wooden houses, plus apartment buildings. My family lived in one of them apartments, a narrow third-floor walk-up with four small rooms. That included the kitchen complete with a few of your regular Brooklyn cockroaches. Didn't bother me. Everyone had 'em.

Them days, go along Brooklyn streets and you'd see tons of little flags with big blue stars in front windows. The flags were saying your family had someone in the war. Some windows had more than one star. There were gold stars too. Gold meant your someone had been killed.

There was this blue star in our window because my

pop was in the merchant marine. He sailed in the convoys going 'cross the North Atlantic bringing war supplies to our troops and allies. That meant we never knew where he was. When he wrote—wasn't often—his letters were censored. Which was because, like people said, "Loose lips sink ships." And let me tell you something—it was true too. Tons of ships were torpedoed by German subs. Wolf packs, they called them. And sailors—gobs of 'em—drowned. So I worried about Pop. A lot.

Oh, sure, I'd see him for a few days every couple of months. But it was always a surprise when he came. He'd be dirty, red eyed, needing a shave, and you wouldn't believe how tired. Most of his leave he just slept, except when he got up to eat apples. He loved apples. Ate 'em like they'd just been invented. Core and all, only spitting out the pips.

When his time was up, he'd sail off. We didn't know where. I don't think Pop knew. Anyway, we weren't supposed to ask.

Still, I was better off than my best friend, Duane Coleman, who we called Denny. This Denny, he never saw his pop 'cause his father—a tailor—was an Eighth Army GI. That's General Infantry. The Eighth was fighting Rommel, the Nazi general, in North Africa. No saying when Mr. Coleman would be home. *If* he came home. All us kids were scared of getting one of them telegrams from the government that began, "REGRET TO INFORM YOU THAT . . ."

Now, I was small, but Denny was smaller. I mean, the guy was waiting for his growth spurt like Dodger fans waited for a pennant. You know, "Wait till next year!"

Denny always had this serious look on his face. Maybe it was his wire-frame glasses, which not a lot of kids wore. Or his slicked-back black hair. Or the white shirt and the bow tie he was always wearing. Red suspenders too. Straps, we called them.

Most mornings I walked to school knowing Denny would be waiting for me in front of Coleman Tailors and Cleaning, his family's business. Going to school, we'd talk about war news, our dads, radio shows we heard.

Big radio fans, most late afternoons we listened to *Jack Armstrong, All-American Boy* and to *Captain Midnight*. Because of those radio shows, me and Denny knew America was swarming with spies. The night before, Sunday, *Suspense* was all about this dog that had been trained to carry messages for a Nazi spy, but turned patriotic for some kid. Pure *wham*.

Point is, a lot of them stories were real stuff. Instance, there were these Nazis that got dropped off at midnight by a U-boat right near Amagansett, Long Island—just miles from Brooklyn. Then they took the Long Island Railroad to the city to do sabotage. Except the FBI caught them. It was true too. You could look it up.

So, see, if Denny and me could have found one spy, just one! Jiminy! It would have been the bestest thing in the whole world. Because, see, Denny and me, we had this secret pact that said we weren't supposed to have no secrets from each other.

Now, also, on the way to school, we always passed this newsstand. It was run by this old blind guy—Mr. Teophilo. Mr. Teophilo sat on a wooden orange crate behind a board set on bricks, which had all these city newspapers—morning and afternoon—spread out. Understand, we wouldn't buy any papers. Just read the headlines. Sure, it was scary stuff, but we wanted to know.

This Mr. Teophilo—don't ask me how, 'cause like I said, he was old and blind—he always knew when we were passing by or standing in front of him. You'd come close and he'd turn in your direction with his eyes closed and his face not shaven so good, with this droopy white mustache. Plus this pure gold chain around his neck. Least Denny and me thought it was pure. Don't ask me why we thought that—we just did.

Anyway, we'd come close and Mr. Teophilo would call out, "Hey, Howie. Hey, Denny. Things are looking good." Or, "Things are looking bad."

Or, like that morning, as I passed him, he said, "Hey, Howie, you're late! And things aren't going too well in North Africa neither."

Except that Monday I was worried about something else besides the war. See, I'd flunked my regular Monday math test so many times my mother said to me, "Howard Bellington Crispers, you get one more failing grade, you can forget about going to Saturday kid movies."

That was serious. The Saturday before, I'd seen Chapter Six of *Junior G-Men of the Air* at the Victory Movie Palace. It ended with this kid hero—Lionel Croft— flying his nifty biplane into a Nazi ambush behind the clouds. I *had* to know what happened.

So there I was walking along, with Lionel Croft and the Monday math test chewing my mind, when suddenly I saw Dr. Lomister, the principal of my school, P.S. 8. And the point is—because this is the way this story really begins—Denny was always saying our principal—this Dr. Lomister—was a Nazi spy.

2

OKAY. Seeing Lomister on the street was like seeing King Kong walk by in his undershorts. Not only was the guy *not* in school, he was standing on a brownstone stoop pressing a doorbell button. The thing was, the way he kept turning around made me think he felt guilty about something.

Lomister was this big galoot, a whole lot taller than the other P.S. 8 schoolteachers, who were all women. Dr. Lomister and the custodian were the only men in our school. Why Lomister was called Doctor, I didn't know. Except it didn't have nothing to do with sick. I mean, the guy should have been a drill sergeant, not a principal. He was that nuts for rules. *All* rules. Let me tell you, that guy knew rules like Brooklyn kids knew how many games the Dodgers were out of first place.

Lomister had rules for everything. No tie, no belt—go sit in his office. Get caught running in the halls or shouting—

go sit in his office. Don't pledge allegiance to the flag right—go sit in his office. Write on the basement floor with chalk—go sit in his office. I don't know. Maybe he just liked company. I mean, nobody wanted to be with him.

See what I'm saying? He was a drill sergeant. Fact, Denny and I used to argue about how come Lomister wasn't in the war.

"Bet you anything he dyed his hair gray so he wouldn't get drafted" was my idea.

"A draft dodger?" Denny said. "Tell me another while that's still warm!"

Denny and me, we talked slang a ton. "Dressing up with words," my mom called it.

Anyway, I said to Denny, "Could be he's the last son of a last son. They don't have to go."

"Yeah," he said, "and your grandma drives a tank. He could've volunteered. My old man's fat, short, and bald, and he's fighting in North Africa right now."

"Well, maybe Lomister's got flat feet," I tried. "Flat feet don't march."

"Money from home, Jackson. He could've joined the navy."

"You're sitting on a block of ice," I shot back.

"Hey," Denny cried, "bet you two Wheaties box tops and six warm Mason Crows, I know what he is."

"Okay, what?"

"He's a spy."

"Tell it to the marines," I said.

After all, like we both knew, at regular Thursday morning school assemblies, Lomister was always giving these boring speeches that "this war is to protect our country. Because our country is run by rules, not men." And that we had to follow the rules for "our boys over there." You know, bunch of patriotic flak.

Thing is, the guy was always making a fuss about how early *he* got to school—before *anyone*, for cripe's sake. I mean, one of his favorite sayings was "You have to start early to bring our boys home early."

Not even my kid sister, Gloria, who drooled over school so much she got there twenty minutes before I did, arrived before Lomister.

But see, there was Lomister, *not* in school. He was on this stoop. Breaking his own rule about being early! And the way he was acting made me remember what Denny said: Lomister was a spy.

So I ducked behind a car to see what was going on.

3

THE FRONT DOOR to the brownstone opened. Whoever opened it stayed in a shadow. That was so suspicious it made me crack my knuckles, which I did whenever I was nervous, though my mother said I'd grow up deformed.

Anyway, next thing, Lomister took off his hat and went inside, shutting the door behind him. Just like the movies.

Now, Lomister went up the front steps—the stoop— that led up to the second floor, where the main door was. But see, next to the stoop was another set of smaller steps that went *down* a little ways to the lowest floor of the house. And next to those steps was a fenced-in place with a steel door that opened to a chute, which was used for delivering coal to the house furnace. Get the picture?

That morning the basement steel door was propped open a couple of inches. Probably because the coal man was coming. The minute I seen that, I knew I could open it more and get into the house and snoop around. And hey, if Lomister was a spy and I could prove it, then Denny and me could tell the FBI. We'd be big-shot heroes with our pictures a front-page extra on the *Brooklyn Eagle*.

But there was a whole other idea which went through my head faster than the lightning that turned Billy Batson into Captain Marvel. It was this: If I got to school late, I wouldn't be able to take the math test. If I didn't take the math test, my teacher, Miss Gossim, couldn't fail me. If I didn't fail the test, my mom couldn't make me miss Chapter Seven of *Junior G-Men of the Air*.

What's more, as I was standing there trying to make up my mind, it started spitting rain.

All of which should explain how come I ran across the street, climbed over the low railing, and lifted that steel door.

I was going inside.

4

OKAY. This chute I told you about was a long U-shaped metal slide, shiny because of all the coal that had slid down. It went from the inside lip of the steel door right on down into the house basement.

So what did I do? I sat on the door frame, legs dangling into the slide, lunch box and satchel under one arm, holding the steel door wide open with my free hand. Then I hitched forward and let go of the door.

Trouble was, the steel door dropped a lot faster than me, so I got me a *bingo-whacko* on the old bean. I'm telling you, sliding down the chute into the basement, I was seeing tons of stars. And all of them were in my head.

Next second I was sitting woozy at the bottom. But light was coming from somewhere, so I could see some stuff. I was in the basement all right. It was long, low, and hot, with stale, dusty air thick as butterscotch pudding. Place smelled rotten too. From garbage, I figured. At the far end were steps leading up, and a weak lightbulb glowing up top.

Next to where I came down was this big, bulky furnace with fat pipes that ran out from its top section. Looked like a giant robot octopus with silver arms. Nearby was a shovel for tossing coal into the firebox. The coal pile was real low. That figured.

Anyway, I was sitting there when the furnace turned on with a roar. Flames licked around the edges of the fire door, throwing out more light. Now I could see stacked cardboard boxes and a workbench with tools. There was an old tennis racquet too, plus a couple of baseball bats. Also some old trunks and suitcases sitting right next to— get this—a couple of filing cabinets.

Now, them file cabinets wowed me. See, from radio shows, movies, and comic books, I knew that private eyes, superheroes, and secret agents *always* found what they called criminal-eating evidence in file cabinets. So there I was, surer than ever I was in a spy nest.

Soon as I got my head back straight, I stood up from the chute and headed for that flight of steps.

Grabbing the shaky banister, I went up. When I reached the top, I put my ear to the door. Didn't hear nothing. I tried the door handle. Wouldn't budge. Hey, more proof that whoever lived in the house had something to hide, right? Over our place we *never* shut doors. "You want to be private," we'd say, "go join the army."

Anyway, the door being shut, I went back down to the basement and tried to think what to do—other than leave. That's when I noticed another door, half the size of an ordinary door. It was set into a wall maybe three feet off the ground. No regular door handle, either, just a latch.

Right below were these garbage cans.

I shoved the cans to one side and tried the door. It was stuck, so I used two hands to yank. *Pop!* It opened! Set into a shaft was a large, tall box with ropes attached to its top. Two more ropes dangled in front of it. A broken dinner plate was lying on the bottom.

What I'd found was a dumbwaiter.

Now, in case you didn't know, dumbwaiters aren't "dumb" like in "stupid," but "silent." They were small elevators used for sending food and stuff from one floor of a house to another. Or they hauled garbage to the basement, which explained how come there were garbage cans down there.

Soon as I understood what I'd found, I got thrilled. See, I figured I could get into the box, pull on the ropes, and get into the house above.

Then I thought, Whoa down! I was chasing Nazi spies. Going up could be dangerous. But right off I said to myself, Hey, Howie, what's more important, math test or spy nest?

Being patriotic, I climbed into the box.

5

LET ME TELL you something, that dumbwaiter wasn't just tight, it stunk to high heaven. I had to sit with my head against my pulled-up knees, fingers of one hand squeezing my nose while my other hand grabbed hold of the rope dangling in front of me. When I jerked the rope down, the dumbwaiter, with me in it, went up.

Now, I have to admit, I worried what would happen if, you know, the ropes broke or the box got stuck. But guess what? Didn't happen. Every time I yanked the rope down, she went up-sa-daisy.

Sure, there was some squeaking. Nothing loud. And whenever I stopped—and it was hard work, so I stopped tons—it stayed put.

Now, soon as I moved out of the basement, everything went dark. *Super* dark. Then, going higher, I saw light seeping through cracks. I kept pulling the rope, coming to a stop only when—*bam!*—I slammed against something.

In front of me was this square line of light. It looked

like a door, so I pushed at it. Wouldn't give. I pushed again. When it still wouldn't budge, I squirmed around, got on my knees. With my body behind me—all seventy pounds—I shoved. The door burst open so quick I plopped onto the floor.

I was lying there trying to catch my breath when I heard a voice.

"This teacher," I heard Dr. Lomister saying—because I could be at the North Pole and I'd still know his voice—"this Miss Gossim, she must be immediately fired."

6

NOW, TO UNDERSTAND this story, you have to know right off that, far as I was concerned, the only thing worth going to school for was this Miss Gossim. Veronica Lake? Betty Grable? Lana Turner? Pretty nifty movie stars. But to me, nothing compared to Miss Gossim.

Miss Gossim was what we called a dilly, a dish, an angel-cake package with tutti-frutti icing on top. Full of smiles too. With frilly blond hair, blue-gray eyes, plus lipstick-red lips. There may have been dirt in the world—wasn't a speckle on Miss Gossim. I mean, she wasn't just clean, she glowed. A regular flower. Like the kind which my class visited on a Brooklyn Botanic Garden field trip.

'Course, she could be strict. No gum chewing. If you were caught chewing, you had to stick the gum on your nose. No note passing. Caught passing a note and she'd read it out loud to the whole class. No writing on your desk neither. Do that and you had to stay after school and get it off. Least her rules made sense, not like Lomister's.

And Miss Gossim liked to laugh a lot. She had one of those laughs that made you join in. Or she said things like "Oh, let's forget long division and tell jokes." She would too.

"Knock knock."

"Who's there?"

"Amos."

"Amos who?"

"Amos-quito bit me."

Miss Gossim was kind, always asking us about our military dads, brothers, sisters, moms. You know, where they were. How they were doing. She even kept a map in the classroom to show it. All them teachers did that, only, see, Miss Gossim wasn't just doing it—she *cared*. So, natch, we told her everything. I mean, that map was telling kids like me I wasn't the only one with family in the war.

Miss Gossim never got mad. Most she'd ever do was look at you sort of sad eyed and say, "Howie, I'm *very* disappointed." 'Course, if she said it, you'd feel worse than a Giants fan in Ebbets Field. I mean, I'd have done anything to get her smile back.

Rolanda was her first name. I heard the school secretary, Mrs. Partridge, call her that. I knew it must be true because she and Miss Gossim were friends. I never heard that name before. But to me, that name, *Rolanda*, was so magic I kept it to myself. Didn't even tell Denny, who, like I said, was my bestest friend with our secret pact about not having secrets. The thing was, when it came to Miss Gossim, things were different.

At night when I was in bed and the lights were out in the room which I shared with my kid sister, Gloria, I'd get to thinking about Denny's dad, or how hard Mom was working at the Navy Yard, or like I said, my math. Or, most of all, I'd worry about Pop sailing by Nazi wolf packs loaded with torpedoes just waiting to ambush him.

Thing is, to get all that stuff out of my head I'd pretend a smiling, perfume-smelling Miss Gossim was leaning over me. Understand? She was my emergency brake, my life raft, my parachute, my own private rescue squad.

"Good-night, Howie Crispers," she'd whisper into my ear.

And I'd look up into those blue-gray eyes of hers and whisper, "Good-night, Rolanda Gossim."

Then, *wham*, like magic, them submarines would sink. The war stopped, Pop was safe, and I could sleep.

Only now Dr. Lomister was going to fire her.

7

ANYWAY, THERE I WAS, in this long, narrow hallway of the brownstone. The only light was coming from a window at the other end. The ceiling was high with some kind of leafy-design plaster molding. On the wall, blue wallpaper with pictures of clouds and birds on it. Hanging from the middle of the ceiling was this chandelier with dangling bits of glass. The light was off.

Looking toward the other end of the hall, I saw the curvy tip of a banister. Which must have belonged to steps leading down. My escape, I figured, if I had to make tracks.

In the middle of the hallway—on the right—was a door. To an apartment, I guessed. At least, Dr. Lomister's voice was coming out from behind it.

Another voice—a lady's—said, "What possible reason is there to fire her?"

"Wilma, I'm not free to say" came Lomister's voice again. "Just take my word for it. She must leave."

I crept closer.

"Gilbert, didn't you tell me that this Gossim woman was one of your best teachers?"

"Teachers," Lomister said, like he was the local Mussolini or something, "must follow rules too."

"Can you find a replacement?"

"We'll manage."

"And what about the children? Will this upset them?"

"They won't care. A teacher is a teacher."

I cracked my knuckles.

"Well, since you've requested it, I suppose I'm willing to act," this Wilma went on. "How much notice are you going to give her?"

"One week. Next Monday will be her last day."

"Gilbert, isn't this unusual? It certainly hasn't happened

since I've come on the job. And in the middle of the term. Plus, I must admit, I'm curious. For you to come here at this hour—"

"It's a very personal matter, Wilma. I have no desire to embarrass the young woman. Besides, she and my secretary are close friends. And may I remind you, there's a war on. Strict moral standards must be adhered to. We must show the children that everybody—even adults—follows established rules."

So this Wilma ups and says, "Very well, Gilbert—if you wish it. I'll send someone to your office this morning with the paperwork."

"It'll be best—"

Now I was listening so hard my big ears were almost inside the apartment. So the second I realized Lomister was coming out, I tore to the end of the hall and dove back into the dumbwaiter. I was just reaching out to pull the door shut when the voices got louder, like they were in the hallway. I snapped my hand in.

"Thank you for coming by," the woman said.

"Wilma," Dr. Lomister said, "I do apologize for coming so early."

"I'll take care of things," the woman said. Then she

said, "Oh, dear. That dumbwaiter door is open. It'll make the hall smell."

"I'll fix it," Dr. Lomister said.

I made a grab at one of the ropes dangling before me and yanked. Instead of going down, the dumbwaiter went up. *Bang!* It smashed into the top of the shaft. I grabbed the second rope with both hands and pulled. This time the dumbwaiter went right. As I dropped, the door above me slammed shut. Everything went dark again.

8

FIGURING IT WAS SAFE, I let go of the rope and I took a deep breath, which was a mistake because I gagged on the garbage stink. But with the dumbwaiter staying put, I sat back. I had to think over what I'd heard.

Miss Gossim was being fired.

Now, don't get me wrong, grown-ups did tons of stuff I didn't understand. And, sure, they were them and I was us. But see, I couldn't figure any way how Miss Gossim could have done something that deserved being fired. Just the idea made me feeble. And as for Lomister saying us kids wouldn't care, that made me furious.

The best I could figure was like this: Lots of radio or movie bad guys fell in love with pretty ladies. When the ladies refused to marry them, the bad guys did something bad to them. Which is why they were bad. But then these good guys came and saved the women and treated them right. Which was why there were good guys. Like me.

And with thousands of guys being drafted into the army and a whole lot of them being killed, good guys like me were getting scarce. The way I figured it, in a few years I'd probably be older. Then I'd marry her.

And the thing was, wasn't the whole war supposed to be about being a free country? Didn't Miss Gossim have the right to do what she wanted?

So sitting there, I made up my mind. It was up to me to do something to make sure Miss Gossim stayed around.

Only thing was, I had to get to school first.

Working the dumbwaiter ropes, I lowered myself down. I squirmed out of the box into the basement. My books and lunch box were where I had left them, right at the bottom of the coal chute. I was just about to climb out when that outside steel door flapped open.

I jumped back. First thing I saw, it was raining hard. Really coming down. Then a voice shouted, "Hey, Rediger! Door's open. Chute's set. Let the coal rip."

Next second motors whirring, gears grinding. Jeepers creepers! A coal truck was dumping coal.

Sure enough, coal chunks came roaring down the chute in a cloud of thick black dust. Then the steel door banged shut and I heard the trunk grind away.

Me? I was spitting and choking. I mean, I was covered with coal dust thick as a fried doughnut with fudge frosting. Worse, when the dust settled, all I could see was this huge pile of coal blocking my way out. Under it was my lunch box and schoolbooks.

I didn't have no choice. I picked up the shovel and started digging.

9

OKAY, WHILE THAT was going on with me, over at P.S. 8, up in Class Five-B, the school day was getting started.

Now, my fifth-grade classroom had these windows on

the street side, windows so big you needed a ten-foot pole to open them. Under the windows was a small bookcase with textbooks. The wardrobe—with its four connected, sliding doors—took up the full length of another wall. That was where we hung our coats and left boots and lunches. The third wall had examples of good penmanship and a map of the world where tiny American flags were stuck.

At the front of the room was the blackboard and an American flag—regular size—hanging from a short pole. The flag was next to pictures of George Washington, Abraham Lincoln, and President Roosevelt. Nearby was a round clock. Its red minute hand always moved in jerks.

Miss Gossim's wood desk was up front and center of the class, covered by this big green inkblotter and a globe. Textbooks were lined up at the desk's front edge. Also, a small glass bottle, which always had a yellow flower sticking out of it, glowing like a bit of sun.

Also, two wooden chairs, one behind her desk, one to the side.

Right in front of Miss Gossim's desk were the kids' desks. Six rows of six desks. Thirty-six of them. Made of wood and cast iron, bolted to the floor. Each one had a hinged wooden seat fixed to the desk behind it. Every desk was grooved on top for pens and pencils. This top lifted up so you could put away books and papers. Had a little glass inkwell too.

Now, like I already told you, I wasn't there, but that day must of started—like every day—with Miss Gossim at the blackboard, putting up the day's date, which, that day, was *March 22, 1943*. On the other side of the blackboard was a list headed TODAY'S MONITORS.

Flag Monitor: Duane Coleman
Attendance Monitor: Gladys Halflinger
Ink Monitor: Betty Wu
Window Monitor: Albert Porter
Scrap Paper Monitor: Toby Robinson
Milk Monitor: Gladiola Alvarez
Eraser Monitor: Howard Crispers
Dismissal Monitor: Tom Ewing

Next to it she had numbered out the day's schedule. Number one was "Math test." See, that stuff stayed on the board all day. Which is how come I can tell you that morning went something like this:

A few minutes after the second bell clanged, the classroom door flung open. Thirty-five kids came tumbling in like gangbusters and raced for the wardrobe, then headed to their desks. Seats dropped, desktops lifted, books got shoved away. Then everybody sat with their feet straight, knees together, hands on top of their desks. Some were dressed pretty good. A lot weren't. The girls wore skirts. The guys had ties.

By the way, if you didn't wear a tie, most teachers stuck a paper—that said TIE on it—on your shirt with a pin. But Miss Gossim had a bunch of real ties for poor kids so they wouldn't get in trouble with Lomister. Like I said, she was a peach.

Anyway, after she took attendance, Miss Gossim said, "I am so glad to see you! I just know we're going to have a fine week. So, once again, good morning, children!"

This time all the kids came back in one ragged voice, "Good morning, Miss Gossim!"

She looked up and down the rows. "I'm so happy none of you are gumdrops," she said, "afraid of melting in the rain. We'll make our own sunny day. But, first things first. Hands out!"

The kids stuck their hands out palms down, over desks. Miss Gossim marched up and down the aisles looking for filth. As she went by, kids flipped their hands over so the other side could be seen.

"Always good, Denny," she said. "Billy Leider, you need to do a better job beneath your nails.

"Excellent," she said when she checked all hands. "Now remember, tomorrow is head-lice examination day. Emily, are you listening? But let's start our day with the Pledge of Allegiance." She turned toward the monitor list.

"Denny, it's your turn to lead us in the pledge. As we all know, Denny's father is with our troops in North Africa. So we know how important this is for him."

Denny went up to the front of the class and in his high-pitched voice said, "Please stand for the pledge."

Seats rattled as kids came to attention. Hands over hearts, they chanted,

"I PLEDGE ALLEGIANCE TO THE FLAG OF THE
UNITED STATES OF AMERICA AND TO THE
REPUBLIC FOR WHICH IT STANDS, ONE NATION,
INDIVISIBLE, WITH LIBERTY AND JUSTICE FOR ALL."

Then the kids dropped down into their desks.

"Betty Wu, you're ink monitor today," Miss Gossim

said. "While you attend to that, I'll hand out the paper for our Monday math test."

This Betty Wu had just come to America from China. You could tell. I mean, she was really polite, always wanting to do the right thing.

Betty went to the back of the room, where she got the glass ink bottle with a steel spout on the top. Holding the bottle carefully, she went around the classroom filling each desk's inkwell. As she did, Miss Gossim passed out sheets of lined paper.

The kids took out their pens.

"We'll start with multiplication," Miss Gossim said. "Problem one."

Suddenly the classroom door swung open. It was me, so soaked with black water I was a walking waterfall, leaving black floods all over the floor.

10

EVERYBODY STARED at me. But I just stood there, dripping.

"Howie," a startled Miss Gossim said, "is that you?"

"Yes, Miss Gossim."

"What happened?"

I looked at her, hardly knowing what to say. I mean, I knew what was going to happen to her before she did.

"Don't you think we should clean you up?" she asked.

"Suppose," I said.

Miss Gossim turned to the class. "I'll need a class monitor."

The hands shot up again. "Me! Me! Miss Gossim, me!"

"Miriam Aresenik," she said. "You can drill everyone in the twelve times tables."

This Miriam—she was tall with red hair in tight braids—came up to the front of the class.

"Now Howie," said Miss Gossim, "leave your lunch box and books here."

Side by side—Miss Gossim keeping her distance—we walked along the hallway until we got to a closet, where she opened the door. The little room was full of mops, brooms, and brushes as well as this big zinc sink. Reaching in, Miss Gossim got some old rags and began to pat me down, starting with my face. As she worked on me, she knelt. I could smell her perfume. And I could see her eyes close up. They were really pretty.

"You were covered with black water when you walked in," she said. "As if you just crawled out of a wet coal mine. Now, Howie," she asked kindly, "what *did* you do to become so filthy?"

I kept thinking about how she was going to be fired. "Wh . . . at?" I said.

"I said you looked as though you just crawled out of a mine. What happened?"

"I . . . I fell into a coal pile."

"Weren't you looking where you were going?" she asked. I think she was trying to keep from laughing.

"I guess not," I said, not knowing how to explain.

She stood up. "Now what do you want to do?" she asked. "Do you want to go home and fetch some dry clothes? Or come to class? It's still raining. Perhaps you'd rather sit by the radiator and dry off."

"I want to stay," I said, afraid she'd be gone and I'd never see her again.

"Good for you!" she said.

Side by side—closer this time—we went down the hall, heading for class.

I was still dripping, but I was trying to find a way to

warn her about what was going to happen. "Miss . . . Miss Gossim," I said a few times.

"Yes, Howie?"

I couldn't get it out. "Thanks for . . . rescuing me," I said.

"You're quite welcome, Howie."

"I know."

Just as we reached the classroom door, she stopped. "Howie, I wish you'd tell me what happened."

"I'm all right," I got out.

She opened the classroom door and we walked in. The kids stared at us.

"Class, I'm afraid Howie got a little wet," Miss Gossim said with a smile. "He needs to sit near the radiator to dry off."

She took up the chair by her desk and carried it to the back of the room.

Grinning, I sat down by the radiator. It was hot and soothing.

Miss Gossim went back to the front of the room. "All right, class," she said. "We were just starting the math test. Howie, now that you're here, I think we should start again. But it might be best if you took the test back there."

My heart sank. I hadn't missed the math test after all.

"Denny, please take your friend paper and pen."

As Denny handed me the paper, his peepers, behind his glasses, were asking me all these questions about what was going on.

"Denny," Miss Gossim called. "Return to your seat, please."

Looking back at me over his shoulder, Denny did like he was told.

"All right, class," Miss Gossim said, "what is five times eight?"

I scribbled 64.

11

WHEN THE MATH test was done, Miss Gossim gave us a stretch time. In the scramble Denny came over.

"What's your story, morning glory?" he said. "How come you didn't meet me going to school?"

"My shoelace broke."

"Horsefeathers," he said. "How'd you get so wet and dirty?"

"Back to seats, please!" Miss Gossim called from the front of the room. "We have a very busy morning."

"I'll tell you during recess," I said.

"Let's take out our geography books," Miss Gossim said. "We were on page forty-two. Argentina. The land of silver."

I started for my desk.

"Howie, are you dry?" Miss Gossim called across the room.

I said, "My shorts is damp."

The class laughed. So did Miss Gossim.

"Well," she said with a big smile, "get your geography book, but stay near the heat."

12

BY TEN-THIRTY snack time I was still by the radiator, pretty well dried out except for my shoes. They were still a little squashy.

About then Miss Gossim checked the clock, set down her copy of our reader, and said, "Class, you may put your books away and fetch your snacks." Then, all of a sudden, she said, "Oh! I completely forgot!"

We looked at her.

She went to the map of the world, which was on the side wall. "We forgot to learn what's happening with our war families," she said.

So, like she did every couple of days, she went round the class, asking each kid what their family was doing for the war.

Billy Wiggins said his father had gone into basic training in South Carolina.

"The Old South," Miss Gossim said, and stuck a little paper American flag on the map.

Margaret Hillers said she thought her father was in England.

"That's Merry Old England," Miss Gossim said with a laugh. "Then we have to move him there, don't we?" She shifted one of the little map flags from the middle of the Atlantic Ocean and put it on the spot marked England.

She went through the whole class that way.

Now, there were kids who didn't have family in the service. Or overseas. Didn't matter. Miss Gossim made out like everyone was doing *something*. For instance, when

Ronnie Estes said his mother was working at this office helping servicemen find missing families, Miss Gossim said that was *very* important and put a flag right on Brooklyn.

"Oh, my," she said, when she'd got an answer from everyone in the room, "this war is so hard on so many." Then she just stood there, staring at the map, as if *she* had family in the war. But the next moment she gave us that great smile of hers and dismissed us for morning snack.

Shoving our books away, we made a rush to the wardrobe. Before I got anywhere, Denny got me.

"You going to tell me what happened to you now?" he said.

"Sure."

"So?"

"I was in a coal pile."

"A *coal* pile?"

"Yeah."

"Whata' you talking about?" he said.

"I was in someone's house," I told him, not sure how much I wanted to explain.

"Whose?" Denny asked, like he was on the *Twenty*

Questions radio show.

I stalled. "Hey, I need to get my snack."

I got my stuff from where I'd dropped it up by the door. But when I opened my lunch box, my sandwich and graham-cracker snack—everything was black with coal dust.

I was still staring at my lunch box, trying to decide what to do, when the classroom door opened. It was Mrs. Partridge, the school secretary. She was this big happy woman. Little kids loved her because she hugged them a lot. Big kids hated her because she hugged them a lot too.

Except that time when she came in, she wasn't looking too happy. Seeing her, my heart sank. I knew what was going to happen.

"Hey, secret pact," I heard Denny say. "You going to tell me what you did?" And he made this mysterious sign we had made up, which was pulling on his right earlobe. It was supposed to mean, "Remember, no secrets."

I didn't answer. Cracking my knuckles, I was watching Mrs. Partridge go up to Miss Gossim.

The teacher was sipping a cup of hot tea, which she did during snack time. Kept it in a vacuum bottle. But seeing Mrs. Partridge, she stood up. There was this smile on her face. Like I told you, they were friends.

I couldn't hear what Mrs. Partridge said. She spoke too low. But the more she said, the more Miss Gossim's smile faded. A hand went to her heart. She even put her teacup down so quick that tea slopped out.

Clearing her throat, she turned to the class. "Attention, children," she called. She was trying to smile and use her bright voice. It didn't work.

"I have to run down to see Dr. Lomister for a moment," she said. "Please take your snacks to your seats."

The class did like she told them.

I hung back, not sure where I was supposed to go.

My being there must have caught Miss Gossim's eye. "Howie," she said, "will you be class monitor? Class, take out your readers, and turn to chapter fourteen. Everyone will take turns reading out loud paragraph by paragraph. Howie—"

She opened the bottom drawer of her desk, took out her purse, and left the room with Mrs. Partridge.

We watched her go.

Now understand, I might have been the only one who knew what was happening, but the other kids were pretty quiet too. They were looking at each other for answers.

In her loud voice, Lucy Amaldi said, "Maybe her

brother was killed in the war."

Wasn't dumb. Three times that year kids in the school had been called to the office because of news like that from home.

Then Denny piped up and said, "She doesn't have a brother."

That took me by surprise. I didn't know that. And if Denny knew, how come he hadn't told me? I mean, what about our no-secrets pact?

"Maybe it was her father," Marcus Sanders said from across the room.

"Her father died a long time ago," Denny said.

"Or her sister?" someone said.

"She doesn't have a sister," Denny told us.

"How come you're such an Abercrombie, knowing so much?" Willa DiSouza demanded.

I was thinking, Good question.

Denny said, "I just do."

The stinker. I was wondering what else he knew. Maybe he knew Miss Gossim's first name too and hadn't told me.

Now, I admit, I could have said what was going on. Only I didn't want to say how come I knew. See, I liked thinking this was something only Miss Gossim and me knew. Understand? Private. Just between us.

Standing in front of her desk, I held up the textbook. "Chapter fourteen," I said. "We're supposed to read."

Denny gazed at me. From his look I could tell he knew I knew more than I was saying, and that my being late that morning had something to do with what I knew. So, staring back, I pulled my right earlobe. Our signal. That way he knew I'd tell him more later. He gave back a pull on his earlobe and turned away.

"Tom Ewing," I said, trying to sound like a teacher, "start reading."

The class opened their books. In a singsong voice, Tom began to read:

"Mr. Brown went to the big power station.
It was very large. It was very powerful.
'Oh, my,' he said. 'This building is big.
It is grand. It is good.'"

It wasn't just boring, it was stupid, that kind of stuff for fifth grade. Even so, Tom and Mr. Brown kept right on going.

13

TWENTY MINUTES AFTER she left, Miss Gossim came back. Right off, you could see something was wrong. Like maybe Joe Louis had just given her a left hook to the head. Sure, she had this smile on, but it didn't look right. Her eyes were misty too.

Me, I'd have bet the whole Brooklyn Bridge, and the Williamsburg one too, Lomister had just fired her.

Soon as she came in, Linda Franklin stopped reading. We all just sat there, staring at her.

Halfway to her desk Miss Gossim's smile got turned off. It switched on again when she held out her hand toward me, asking for the reader.

"Thank you, Howie," she said softly. "I'm sure you did a good job."

I hustled back to my desk, checking her once, twice, over my shoulder. Not looking where I was going, I banged into Natalie Brickle's desk. "Sorry," I mumbled.

The class laughed.

But when I sat down, Miss Gossim was still standing in front of her desk. The look on her face wasn't what you'd call peachy cream-o. Not that I could tell what she was thinking.

All of us were quiet, watching her close, waiting for her to say something.

She smiled again. Sort of.

"Well, then," she finally said, "thanks for being such good children. I appreciate that. My meeting with Dr. Lomister was important, but . . ." She stopped. "But . . . now we have to get on with your education."

She turned to the blackboard and the doings list. "We were going to have music this afternoon. I think we should do it now. I certainly could use some. Please take out your songbooks."

Everybody knew we weren't getting the straight skinny. Even so, we did what we were told.

She said, "Let's start with . . . page twelve, 'O Bright and Shiny Day!'" She picked up her pitch pipe from her desk and gave this long, high note.

At first we sang quietly. Pretty soon we were tooting along like a bunch of taxicabs in a Times Square traffic jam.

14

BY LUNCHTIME Miss Gossim was acting mostly like her old self again. Full of smiles, you know, pep. Sure, I think we all knew it was phony, but the class went along. You know, pretend normal. We were good at that.

Anyway, about an hour later we were dismissed for lunch hour, which was, actually, only half an hour. The class marched out in line. They followed our monitor, who that day was Billy Leider—the kid with dirty nails. Since it was still raining, we went down to the basement.

On days it didn't rain, we went out to the yard. But on rainy days some eight hundred kids stuffed themselves in the basement. The place wasn't big either. But us kids—little bitty kindergartners up to lumpy eighth graders—swarmed in, stinking the place up with sweat, wet wool, and sour milk. We'd play games, eat our lunches, or go tearing around the place like the screaming meemies.

With its cement floor and low ceiling, the place

became one big, steamy, smelly, sweat hole. You had to shout to make yourself heard. Kids eating lunches everywhere. Food all over the floor. Boys playing kick ball, tag ball, dodgeball, ring-a-lievo, dump the chump, the regular stuff. A few brave girls played with them. The rest of the girls, if they were playing anything, were jumping rope, doing jacks, hopscotch.

Sure, there were a few teachers trying to keep order. But it was like trying to stop a leaky bucket that had fourteen holes and you had only what? Maybe two fingers.

Okay. Denny and me, we went to our regular eating place. It was up against one of the gray concrete walls, near a storage bin. A good spot 'cause it was hard to play anything there. Quieter too.

"My sandwich got coal dusted," I told him when we settled in. "You got anything extra?"

He opened his lunch box. He had this apple, and a jelly sandwich that looked like a bad scab, plus a Twinkie and a box of Mason Dots.

"You can go halvsies on my sandwich," he said. Ripping his scab sandwich in half, he checked sizes and gave me the bigger piece. "You going to tell me what happened now?" he asked.

Mouth full, I said, "Swear not to tell?"

"Sure."

Now in them days, when you made a swear, you had to do it right. Otherwise, it wasn't no good. So I made my right hand into a fist except for my pinky, which I stuck out.

Denny did the same, hooking his pinky around mine. "First one who snitches drops dead and no fins," I said, giving the regular warning against busted swears or behind-the-back crossed fingers—"fins"—which made a swear no good.

"First one who snitches drops dead and no fins," he repeated. Then he did the formal chop to pull our hands apart.

So I told Denny everything I'd done and heard in the morning.

He listened good, eyes staring at me from behind his specs. A couple of times his bow tie bobbed.

When I was done, he said, "Miss Gossim got . . . *fired?*"

"Swear to God."

"When's her last day?"

"Next Monday."

"Winkin' willies." He fiddled with his suspenders a bit. "But . . . how come?"

I gave him my idea about Lomister being mad at her because she wouldn't marry him.

"Oh, wow, you really think so?" he said.

"Could be."

"Think Lomister's that mean?"

"Yeah."

"A thing like that, though, you gotta be sure."

"Well, then," I said, wanting to show off, "I'll ask."

"Ask who?"

"Miss Gossim."

"No you won't."

"Yes I will."

"I dare you. Double dare! Triple dare."

"What do you bet?"

"My new Captain America comic book."

"Done."

"Swear!" Denny held up his fist again, pinky out. We made another vow.

Then he said, "How you going to?"

"I'm blackboard eraser monitor."

Being eraser monitor meant you stayed after school a bit.

He looked at me. "You really going to?"

I said, "Cross my heart and hope to die."

15

BY THE END of the day, Miss Gossim was in a pretty good mood. Ten minutes to three she said it was room-cleaning time.

We packed up, saving the scrap paper for the war effort. Hats, coats, and other stuff was pulled from the wardrobe. Then everybody except me lined up by the door, ready to go.

At the doorway, just before going out, Denny turns back to look at me, pulls his earlobe.

I did the same.

No secrets.

When the final bell rang, the class marched out. The dismissal monitor—Tom Ewing—led the way. I was the only kid left.

While Miss Gossim sat at her desk and went through papers, I got the eraser box from inside the wardrobe, picked up the erasers from the blackboards, and took 'em out to the school yard. The rain had stopped, but it was gray.

A game of baseball was going on with a tape ball and a broomstick. A few girls were doing hopscotch. I joined up with the kids from other classes who were working their classroom erasers.

You cleaned erasers by holding one in each hand. Sticking your arms out as far in front of you as you could, you closed your eyes, then clapped the erasers together to beat out the chalk dust. Like making clouds.

Not wanting to have Miss Gossim walk out on me, I worked fast. I mean, I might have been scared—and I was—but I had to get some answers.

I went back to the class. In the morning I had come in all black. In the afternoon, all white. When I walked in, she was still at her desk, pencil in hand, papers in front. Only she was staring off somewhere. I wondered where.

I went round and put the clean erasers where they were supposed to go, on the ledges at the bottom of each blackboard. Then I just stood by the door, waiting for her to notice me. Finally, I cracked my knuckles.

She looked up, gave me a quick smile, and said, "Thank you, Howie," before going back to her work.

Now the thing was, I was supposed to leave. Only, see, I didn't. I kept standing there, halfway between her desk and the door.

Finally, I said, "Miss . . . Gossim . . ."

She glanced around. "Yes, Howie?" she said, surprised, I think, I was still there. "Is something the matter?"

"I . . . I'm . . . I'm sorry about . . ."

"Sorry, Howie? About what?"

"Your being . . . being . . . fired," I blurted out.

She gasped. "How do you know about that?" she whispered.

Not expecting the question, I just stood there.

She said, "Does the whole class know?"

"Just . . . me," I said, skipping over the Denny part.

"How did you learn?" she asked.

"Miss Gossim," I said, "remember how I came late to school this morning?" I wasn't looking at her. Just staring at my shoes like they were a dollar bill I'd found on the curb.

"You were covered with coal soot."

"Well, see, I was digging my way out of a coal pile."

Her brow wrinkled. "I don't understand."

I took a deep breath, looked up, and said, "Miss Gossim, it was like this. . . ." Then I blurted out what happened that morning. The whole thing. How I went into the house. Going up the dumbwaiter. Hearing Lomister. Digging out.

The more I talked, the bigger her blue-gray eyes got. Couple of times I was pretty sure she was going to laugh. Only she didn't. And when I told her all the talk I heard— you know, between Lomister and that woman named Wilma—she got pretty serious.

She said, "That must have been Mrs. Wolch."

"Who's Mrs. Wolch?"

"She's acting superintendent of schools."

"What's that?"

"Dr. Lomister's superior. His boss."

"Oh."

"And you were *there*?" she said, sort of, I guess, still amazed.

"Sure. One-seventy-two Hicks Street."

Miss Gossim got thoughtful. Then I saw her write

down the address I just said.

"So that's how I know," I muttered.

"Did you hear Dr. Lomister say *why* I was being fired?" She looked sad.

"No."

I waited for her to tell me why, but when she didn't I said, "I'm really sorry. Are . . . are you . . . mad at me or anything?"

Miss Gossim looked at me with faraway eyes. "No," she said. "Of course not."

Then she took a deep breath and said, "Howie, I really don't understand. Why did you even go into Mrs. Wolch's house?"

"Denny Coleman is always saying Dr. Lomister is a spy."

"A *spy*?" she cried.

"Yeah. They're all around, you know."

"Howie, I don't believe Dr. Lomister is a spy," she said, adding, "or for that matter anyone in our school."

"You don't?" I said, disappointed.

"Not at all."

I waited for her to say something more. When she didn't, I said, "Miss Gossim . . ."

"Yes, Howie?"

"Then how come . . . I mean, how come you're being fired?"

She turned away.

So I said, "Well, I just wish you weren't."

She came back to me with that sad look on her face. "Thank you, Howie," she said. "I wish I weren't either."

"Can I do something about it? Help you or anything?"

"Howie, you're very sweet to offer. I can't imagine how you could. Besides, this is something I need to work out for myself. Except, may I ask you, please, don't tell the class what you know. Can you promise me that?"

"Yes, Miss Gossim," I said, which wasn't honest, 'cause, see, I told Denny already.

She said, "Thank you. I appreciate it. Now, it's late. You'd better go on home."

I headed for the door.

"Howie!" she called.

"Yes, Miss Gossim."

She picked up a paper from her desk. "I'm afraid you failed the math test again."

"Miss Gossim," I cried, "if I fail, my mom said she won't let me go to the Saturday movies. It's Chapter Seven, *Junior G-Men of the Air!*"

She broke into a smile. "Oh, dear. That *is* serious. Then let's see. Can you promise me you'll study real hard tonight? If you do, I'll give you another test tomorrow. I think everyone deserves a second chance. Don't you?"

"Yes, Miss Gossim."

"Good-night, Howie."

"Good-night, Miss Gossim."

16

DENNY WAS WAITING for me on the front school steps. "You talk to her?" he said soon as he saw me.

"Yeah. You owe me a comic book."

We started walking up Hicks Street slowly. After a while, he said, "Hey, what about our no-secrets pact?"

"I know. Just thinking."

"Less thinking, Jackson. More talking. What'd you say to her?"

"Said I knew she'd been fired."

"What'd she say?"

"Wanted to know if everybody knew. Said I didn't think so. I didn't say I told you."

"How come?"

"Just didn't."

"You say anything else?"

"I said, you know, 'How come?'"

"How come what?"

"How come she got fired."

"What she say?"

"She didn't."

"You say anything else?"

"Said I'd like to help her."

"What she say then?"

"Said I shouldn't."

"Are you gonna?"

"Maybe."

"How?"

"Don't know."

"You say that to her?"

"No."

"What about spies? You say anything about them?"

"Yeah."

"What she say?"

"Said she didn't think there were any."

"Oh."

"But you know what?"

"What?"

"I really like her."

"So do I."

"You do?"

"Yeah."

"Oh."

We walked on without more talking, stopping only to stare at the afternoon headlines at old Mr. Teophilo's. But I wasn't thinking about the war. I was looking at Denny sort of sideways. Thing is, and I admit it, I was jealous. See, I'm thinking, how come my best friend has to like Miss Gossim too? He could have picked someone else. And then, all of a sudden, I started worrying. What if she liked him better?

But right about then Denny said, "You went into that house thinking about spies, right?"

"Yeah."

"You still think it has anything to do with that?"

"No."

"How come?"

"The lady Lomister was talking to was the acting superintendent of schools, that's all. Her name is Mrs. Wolch."

"How do you know who it was?"

"Miss Gossim told me."

"Why Lomister go to her?"

"Mrs. Wolch is his boss."

"I didn't know he got a boss."

"Everybody got a boss."

"God don't."

"God ain't everybody."

"Pretty much."

"Come on, Denny, that's nothing to do with what we're talking about."

Denny got quiet. Then he said, "We going to do some collecting?"

Denny and me—like tons of kids—went around the neighborhood getting newspaper, scrap metal, and old clothes—stuff, see, for the war effort. He had an old wagon—a red Radio Flyer—which was great for hauling.

We'd store whatever we got over at his place. Every couple of weeks we'd bring it to the collection center at Brooklyn Borough Hall.

"Thing is," he said, "we could go to that house you were at too. Maybe learn more about what's going on."

"That Mrs. Wolch's?"

"Yeah."

"Spy on it?"

"Sure. Where's it at?" he asked.

"One-seventy-two Hicks." I looked at him. "Why do you think she got fired?"

"Hey, Jackson," he said, "don't you know there's a war on?"

17

AFTER DENNY AND I agreed to meet at his house, I went home to get out of my school clothes and to make sure my kid sister, Gloria, was all right.

Gloria was two years younger than me. With braids and bangs, she was always wanting to know what I was doing. Or tagging after me and my pals. Far as I was concerned, she was a drizzle puss.

But looking after Gloria was something I was supposed to do ever since my mom started working at the Navy Yard. She left before we went to school and didn't get home till night, around six-thirty.

"I don't want to take care of her," I told my mom.

"Howard Bellington Crispers," she said, "don't you know there's a war on?"

See. You couldn't say nothing to that.

Gloria liked radio soap operas. Liked them more than anything else in the world. There were tons of them too. *The Romance of Helen Trent, Our Gal Sunday, Backstage Wife.* Gloria breathed all that lovey-dovey-oolie-droolie-behind-the-back stuff like other people breathed air. So what Gloria would do, see, is rush home after school and paste herself to the radio. Which was fine with me. That way I could do what I wanted.

So that afternoon, by the time I got home, Gloria was in the kitchen, listening to *Linda's First Love.* This was—and I kid you not because I ain't forgot—"About a Girl in Love with the World around Us, and in Love with Wealthy Young Kenneth Woodruff." It all took place in a "midsized city in Indiana."

As Gloria listened, she read one of her Little Orphan Annie books. Don't ask me how she could do both things at once. She just did. It drove me nuts.

I swallowed a glass of Ovaltine, then started out.

"Where you going?" she asked.

"Nowhere."

"Doing what?"

"Nothing."

"Who with?"

"None of your beeswax."

"Can I come?"

"Nope."

She stuck her tongue out at me.

Like I said, looking after my sister was a pain.

18

DENNY WAS WAITING for me with his wagon in front of his family's tailor shop. He was in his school duds—bow tie, suspenders, the works. "My mother said I have to be back by five to mind the store," he explained.

"Okeydokey with me," I said.

"Better do some collecting first," he suggested. "It'll make things look right when we get to that lady's house."

We set off, pulling his noisy wagon behind us. Down the block was a house with two blue stars in the window. It was always worth asking at those places. I went up the stoop and rang the bell.

A window on the first floor slid open. This gray-haired lady stuck her head out.

"Ma'am," I called, "we're collecting scrap for the war effort."

She gave us a smile. "Good boys. Just a moment. I'll check."

Couple of minutes later she came back. She had an old dented kettle and a bundle of newspapers tied with lots of string. She said, "I have two boys in the service."

"Yes, ma'am."

By the time we got to Mrs. Wolch's place, we had three piles of newspapers, a ball of string, two old sweaters, a paper bag full of squashed tin cans, and that kettle. A better haul than most days. But it was getting late.

All of a sudden Denny said, "Cheese it!"

"What?"

"Look." He pointed. Coming up the street was Miss Gossim. She was wearing a brown coat and a hat on her head with a feather. She was walking fast too, head bent, like she was thinking hard about something. Every once in a while she looked at a piece of paper she had in her hand, then up at the houses, like she was checking for an address.

I was thinking, I bet I know what she's doing.

I didn't have to say it out loud. Denny whispered, "Bet you anything she's going to the same place we were going."

I knew she was. Because I gave her the address.

We ducked behind a car to watch. Sure enough, Miss Gossim went up the stoop of 172 and rang the bell. She stood there fidgeting, but never turned around to look our way either.

After maybe ten minutes—and no one coming to the door—she left the stoop and went off the way she came.

Denny started to follow.

"Hold it," I said, grabbing his arm.

"What's the matter?"

"We can't follow someone and drag a wagon full of junk too."

"Why not?"

"Junk ain't private. She'll see us. Or hear us."

"Howie, I can't leave it."

"I'll go alone. Anyway, you said you had to be home by five."

Denny looked at me suspicious. "You promise to tell me everything what happens?"

"Sure."

"I mean it. *Everything*. No secrets, right?"

"No secrets," I said back.

"And no fins," he said, holding out his pinky.

"No fins."

We linked and chopped fast. "See you tomorrow on the way to school," I said, racing off. "And don't worry. I'll tell you everything."

"You better!" he said, but by then I was running to catch up with Miss Gossim. I looked back once. Denny was pulling on his ear.

I didn't. Truth is, I hadn't been fair to Denny. I wasn't worried about the wagon. I wanted to be the only one saving Miss Gossim.

19

OKAY. I followed Miss Gossim as she went along Hicks Street, then made a turn onto Orange Street. I was about half a block behind. She didn't turn around. Not once.

After a while she got to this street called Columbia Heights. It was sort of a cliff that overlooks New York Harbor. There were tons of houses there, but between some of them you could see the harbor. All these boats. Navy ships, cargo boats, tugs, and ferries. Plenty of them.

Behind them was Manhattan with its tall buildings, including the Empire State Building. It was huge, but people said it was mostly empty. Go figure.

Anyway, Miss Gossim was leaning on a fence facing the harbor. Like she was staring at something.

I suddenly got this thought: Maybe she's gonna kill herself. You know, leap off the cliff. Holy smoker-eeno! *Suicide!* Which, see, I happened to know—'cause Denny once told me—was against the law.

I just stood there, heart beating like crazy, not knowing what to do. Except, after a while, Miss Gossim turned. Anyway, she began to walk back along Orange Street, where she went into an apartment house.

I hung back for a while, making sure she really went in. Then I took myself into the building. A quick peek told me she wasn't in the lobby or nothing. But I saw this up-and-down line of mailboxes in the wall with a call button and name label under each box. At the bottom of Apartment 5-C, fifth button down, it said, GOSSIM.

When I went home, I walked right by Coleman Tailors. I didn't talk to Denny. Then, at my house, we didn't have a phone, so I couldn't call neither.

See, I had to think it out in my own head first. You know, before it went into someone else's head.

Only at night, when I got into bed and the lights were out, I couldn't fall asleep. It was like a stuck movie: Miss Gossim just looking over that cliff. It was probably the most awful thing I had seen in my whole entire life.

"Good-night, Rolanda Gossim," I kept saying. But she didn't show up. Not at all.

American Drive Forges Ahead.
Rommel in a Vise.

Grand Admiral Doenitz,
Nazi Germany's Submarine War Wizard,
Pledges U-boat Warfare
Backed by Total Nazi Sea Power.
U-boat Toll Rises As Nazis Use New Tactics.

Test of Army Air Raid Signals
in City Is Set for Wednesday Night.

20

THE NEXT DAY, far as I could see, Miss Gossim was acting normal. Full of smiles and fun. But, see, maybe because I knew what was going on, every once in a while I'd catch her staring out the window. It was as if something was out there only she could see. I checked. Nothing there but Hicks Street.

Miss Gossim let me take the math test again during first recess time, which I did. She graded it right away. I passed it—with a D-minus. Have to admit, I was happy. At least I'd be able to go to the movies next Saturday morning.

But I wondered if her passing me meant she liked me special. Know what I'm saying? Only, when I was watching her, seemed to me she liked all the kids.

Oh, yeah. Another thing happened that day. Like Miss Gossim promised, it was head-lice-check day. The whole room passed. Even Emily. Which was a good thing, because no one liked a louse.

But then Miss Gossim reminded us that next week would be ringworm-check day.

And I was thinking, great, Miss Gossim wouldn't be around. Not even for ringworms.

Allies Lost Millions of Tons
of Shipping in 1942.

Seamen from U.S. Cargo Vessel
Torpedoed in the Atlantic.

Nazi U-boat Menace Is Seen as
Sole Threat to Allied Victory.

To Save Gas, States Asked to
Keep 35-Mile Speed.

21

WEDNESDAY WAS A big day. In school, not much happened. After school, tons.

First, like I was supposed to, when school was over I headed home. Denny had to go somewhere. On the way I checked the headlines. As I was looking at them, old Mr. Teophilo—the blind newsman—turned toward me with his closed eyes and wrinkled eyelids and said, "I don't know, Howie. Looks pretty bad today." He fingered his gold chain like it was some good-luck charm. "Where's Denny today?"

"Had to do something. Mr. Teophilo," I said, "you mind my asking? How come you knew he wasn't here with me?"

"Aw, Howie, it ain't so hard. Everybody is all kinds of different ways. You know, different breathing, talking, moving. They even smell their own way. In the whole world, no two people the same."

I said something like "Yeah," wondering, as always, how he knew.

Soon as I got back to our apartment, Gloria said, "Guess what?"

"What?"

"Letter from Pop." She held up a blue square of paper. It was folded-over thin blue paper to save weight. It was a what we called V—for "victory"—letter.

Near our address on the front was a red stamp mark that read,

CENSORED!

Now, understand, my pop had been gone for more than a month. I was missing and worrying about him a whole lot, so I was pretty pink to see that letter. But the rule in our place was, Only Mom could open his letters. So we left it on the kitchen table by the saltshaker, where she always checked for them.

With Gloria plugged into the radio and reading a book, I went over to a friend's house. The weather being good, a bunch of us played stickball in the middle of the street.

One guy was amazing. He could hit the ball really far.

And let me tell you, that ball was dead, being made of wound-up electrical tape. Still, every time, triple or homer.

Anyway, we had a good time, and I didn't think about my pop or Miss Gossim, not even once. It was kind of a relief.

When I got back home—maybe six-thirty—Mom was there. She looked beat, the way she usually did when she got home from the Navy Yard. Her job was to put in rivets in armor plate on ship repairs. She said it was hard, dull work. But she was forever saying she had to do it right. What if the work was done bad? Think of the lives that could be lost! It could even be Pop.

For instance: She was always telling us this story about a fighter pilot who got shot down in the Pacific. He lived because he clung to his life preserver. Okay. But see, it turned out it was his own mother who packed that preserver in some factory somewhere. Hey, Ripley's Believe It or Not. You could look it up.

So, anyway, when I got back, Mom was at the kitchen table reading Pop's letter. Gloria was sitting beside her.

"Hi," Mom said, as I walked in. "Where you been?"

"Playing ball. What did Pop say?"

"You can read it for yourself while I make dinner."

She put the letter down and opened the cabinet door over the sink. "We'll have ravioli and peas," she said. Took down a couple of cans, staring at them sort of tired. "Even canned goods are rationed now," she said.

"We're out of milk," my sister said.

Mom said, "Fetch my purse and ration book, and get some from the store."

"You don't need ration stamps for milk," I reminded her.

She smiled. I could tell, something in Pop's letter had got to her.

"Why can't Howie get the milk?" Gloria said.

"Because I asked you to."

"Can I get a penny candy?" she asked.

"No," Mom said. "Dinner be ready soon. Now scoot." She opened the two cans and dumped the insides in pots.

I spread my pop's letter before me. Holes had been cut into it. You know, the censor slicing things out he didn't think Pop should be saying. What people called a "Swiss-cheese letter."

Dear Lois and kids,

    Well, I got to   Pretty   crossing.

    We   ships. The Germans were
thick as sharks.

                 is built on a hill. The docks are
old but amazing. Lots of Irish live here. The
Germans bomb a lot, even the cathedral. But we're
safe. We're not waiting for a convoy but heading
right back. I should be home for

             Hope so. I could use some sleep.
And decent grub.

        Your loving husband and father,

        Mitch/Pop

I read the letter a few times, trying, you could guess,
to figure out what the cutout words were.

"Where do you think he is?" I said to my mom when I
couldn't figure it out.

"Sounds like Liverpool," she said.

"Where's that?"

"England."

"It's called Merry Old England," I corrected. "When
do you think he'll be home?"

"Easter, I'm guessing."

"Why would they cut *that* out?"

"If the Germans knew when he hoped to be home, maybe they could figure out when he was leaving and where he'd be. Those U-boats could be right there, waiting for him."

"Then how come he isn't waiting for a convoy? Isn't it safer?"

"Yes."

"Does that mean his ship will be all alone?" I asked, horrified.

"Howie, honey," she said, softly, "I don't know any more than you do."

"But if his ship's alone . . . ," I started to say.

"Howie, it's really better not to talk about—"

All of a sudden air raid sirens started howling.

In case you didn't know, I'll explain. Sirens meant the whole city was supposed to douse lights. Called a blackout. It was to make sure enemy airplanes or ships couldn't home in on us.

Now, for all I knew, maybe enemy planes *were* coming. Hey, they did at Pearl Harbor. It would take plane spotters—up on roofs—to know for sure. To help, there were all these searchlights flicking back and forth against the sky. So we took the siren seriously. In fact, Mom had been holding a pot in her hand. When the sirens came, she dropped the pot on the stove.

After that she didn't seem worried. Not that she would have let on. "Supper will have to wait," she said, turning off the kitchen light. "Howie, go get the front lights."

I hurried down the hall.

"And Howie," she called after me. "When you get everything, go after Gloria. She doesn't like being alone in the blackouts."

I got our apartment dark. Then I made my way out onto the street. Most lights were already off. They would stay that way for an hour, till the all-clear siren.

A few people went scurrying by, trying to get inside. Unless you were in the Civil Defense, you weren't supposed to be on the streets.

As I stood there in front of our building, the last lights on the block went off. No people or cars either. Except for the sirens, the city was quiet, spookylike. Another world. I could even see stars. I liked that part. Until blackouts I'd never really seen stars.

Pretty soon the air raid wardens came down the middle of the street. They wore white armbands and helmets with the Civil Defense insignia. Two of them had walkie-talkies. Their job was to make sure everything was dark. They could arrest you if you made any trouble.

Before they could tell me to get back inside, I headed for the grocery store. It was only three blocks away.

The store, which was pretty small, was mostly dark, except for this tiny burning candle. On the walls were wooden shelves. Not a lot of stuff on them because of all the food shortages. There was an icebox too, for eggs and milk. The potato box was empty. Just a sign that said,

NO POTATOES—SHORTAGES

On one wall was a big poster, which I liked looking at. It was a picture of this blond lady, only she didn't have too much on—just a red, white, and blue sort of flag scarf. She was riding this huge falling bomb. In big letters 'cross the top, it said,

BUY WAR BONDS FOR BOMBS!

Gloria was in the store, clutching a milk bottle. She was sitting next to Mrs. Hakim, who ran the store with her husband. This Mrs. Hakim was a tiny, big-eyed woman.

She always reminded me of a sardine.

"Howie," Mrs. Hakim said soon as she saw me. "Your sister was afraid to go home. I told her she could stay. Now go along, honey. Say hello to your mother for me."

We started home.

"Howie, are we going to be bombed?" Gloria asked as we walked along.

"Shh!" I said, as if some Nazi might hear us.

"Are we?" she whispered

"Nah," I said. "The coast patrol would spot any Germans and shoot them down first. Besides," I told her, "Germans don't have any long-range bombers. Nothing to cross the Atlantic, anyway."

That made her feel better. "Here," she said, giving me the milk. "You carry it. I don't want to drop it."

Every once in a while her hand brushed up against me. Just to feel better, I think.

We passed another air raid warden. "Hey, kids," he yelled, "get on home now. You're not supposed to be out."

Gloria grabbed my hand and made me go faster. But when we reached our building, I said, "Take the milk inside."

"Aren't you coming in?"

"Want to sit and see what's happening. Tell Mom I'll be up soon as it's over."

She gave me this worried look.

"I'll be all right," I told her. "Go on."

She went. I stayed where I was. Way overhead I could see these searchlight beams going back and forth in the sky. Made me think of dueling swords in a Douglas Fairbanks movie.

Another warden went by, but when she gave me this dirty look, I said, "I live here." So she kept going.

But the next warden who showed up stopped right in front of me. "Hey, kid!" he yelled. "What do you think you're doing?"

"I live here," I told him.

He considered me for a moment, then said, "Want to do something useful?"

"Sure," I said.

"My walkie-talkie is on the blink. I'm supposed to report to the section commander—Mr. Handler—that this ward is fine. He's at the corner of Hicks and Orange. Know where that is?"

"Sure."

"Fine. Go on down there and tell him that Watkins of

Ward Sixteen said we're pretty perfect. Repeat that."

"Watkins said Ward Sixteen is pretty perfect."

"Right. And if anyone stops you, just tell him Watkins sent you. Get that?"

"Okay."

"Okay, scoot!"

"Yes, sir." I was on my feet and running. The thing is, I knew I was heading right near where Miss Gossim lived.

22

IT WAS DARK, but I was going the way I went to school. So I reached the corner of Hicks and Orange fast.

The CD commander was easy to find 'cause there was this car, a Packard, with a Civil Defense flag flying from the antenna. A bunch of wardens were hanging around.

"What you doing here, kid?" someone called when I got close.

"I'm supposed to tell Mr. Handler that Watkins said Ward Sixteen is pretty perfect."

"I'm Mr. Handler," said this man from the front seat of

the car. A cigarette was in his mouth. It was stuck in a holder the way I'd seen pictures of President Roosevelt smoking his cigarette.

I gave the message again, adding, "Watkins's walkie-talkie ain't working."

"Yeah. All right, kid. Thanks. Now just beat it home. You're not supposed to be out. You'll get into trouble."

I backed away from the car and the CD men. But instead of going home, I headed for Miss Gossim's apartment building.

I reached it easy. When I got there, all I did was stand outside and look up toward the fifth floor. But since every window in the whole building was dark, I couldn't see nothing.

Even so, it felt good being there. As if I was watching over Miss Gossim or something. I mean, that looking over the cliff like I'd seen her do, it kept coming back bad into my head.

And I kept thinking, Why does she have to get fired?

Anyway, standing there, pretty soon I got to imagining bombs falling and that I had to save her like in the movie *The Masked Marvel*. I'd just burst through smoke and flames, finding her asleep in bed, when I heard, "Hey, kid!"

It was another warden. Some 4-F fat guy, in a helmet and trench coat with a big nose and a mustache, so he looked like an old walrus. He was holding this billy stick like cops carried.

"What do you think you're doing, kid?" he asked, pointing his stick right at me. "You're supposed to be inside. Where do you live?"

I didn't want no trouble. "There," I said, and pointed to Miss Gossim's building.

"Then get yourself inside or I'll book you," he said, taking a step toward me, tapping that stick in the palm of his hand. Showing me what he might do to me.

Scared, I pushed through the heavy glass and iron doors of Miss Gossim's apartment building. It was pretty dark inside. But, see, I figured I could just stay there until the guy left. I turned and looked back. The warden was still there, probably glaring at me, watching and waiting to see if I was really going inside.

What else could I do? Thinking of that billy stick, I counted down five apartment buttons and pushed the one for Miss Gossim's apartment—5-C.

"Who is it?" A voice came from a squawk box next to the door. It might have been rough and crackling, but it was Miss Gossim's voice all right.

Guessing there was a microphone somewhere, I called, "It's me, Howie!"

"Howie?"

"Howie Crispers."

For a moment she didn't say nothing. I snitched another look over my shoulder. The warden must have been going izzy-wizzy at me with his eyes.

"Did you want to see me?" Miss Gossim asked. There was puzzle in her voice.

"Miss Gossim," I shouted. "I got caught outside in the blackout. A warden is saying I have to get off the street right away."

All I heard was silence. I figured she was thinking what to do. Behind me the warden was going *smack*, *smack* into his hand with his billy stick.

Then the door buzzer rang, unlocking the door. I flung myself against it, and it opened.

Okay. I was in this lobby. I could see that much. But I wasn't sure what to do next. It was a blackout. And I wasn't home where I should be but in this building where I shouldn't. And now Miss Gossim was expecting me.

I remembered her apartment was on the fifth floor.

Five-C, right? So I looked around and was able to make out some steps in the back. Holding on to the banister, I started up. And all the time my heart was going *pita-pat*, *pita-pat*. And I'm thinking, *Holy mackerel!* I'm visiting Miss Gossim!

23

WHEN I GOT to the fifth floor, I heard Miss Gossim's voice say, "Howie?"

She was standing in her doorway, holding this lit candle. The flame filled her face with gold. And I was looking at her. She was in this blue bathrobe. I mean, a pinup, for cheese sake! Only *real*. I stood kind of frozen, staring at her, my lips glue-stuck, not knowing what to say.

"Howie?" she called again. "Is that really you?"

"Yes, Miss Gossim."

"Better come in," she said.

When I did like she told me, she stepped aside to let me pass. She closed the door behind us.

It was a tiny place. I mean, a one-room apartment with

a Murphy bed—which was pulled down—an electric cooking plate on a little table, a low table before the bed, plus a folding chair. Maybe a few books. Nothing much else. There must have been a bathroom somewhere. I didn't see it. As for her, like I said, she looked the same, only different. I mean, she seemed smaller than she was in class. Prettier too. Could have been the bathrobe. And with no makeup, her face seemed softer. But mostly she was looking puzzled.

She put her candle on the low table, sat at the end of the Murphy bed, and sort of pointed to the chair. "You can sit," she said. "There's not much room in here."

As I sat, I saw this picture on the low table. It was a guy—just his head—wearing an Army Air Force cap.

"Now, Howie," Miss Gossim said in the same easy low voice she used at school. "What are you doing here? Shouldn't you be home?"

"Well . . . ," I said, not knowing how to explain. Understand, I was embarrassed, but see, excited too. I mean, you know, there I was in Miss Gossim's house. I kept thinking, Wait till I tell Denny!

She said, "Does your mother know where you are?"

I shook my head.

"Oh, dear. And I don't have a phone."

"We don't neither," I said. "It broke. They haven't fixed it yet."

"It takes a long time." She looked at me for a while. "Howie," she asked, "were you coming to visit me?" In the candlelight I could see there was this smile on her lips.

"Not exactly," I said, starting to feel like a moron. "See, after the sirens went off, I had to go out to get my sister because she gets scared—we ran out of milk—and then this warden—his walkie-talkie was broken or something—asked me to give a message to the head warden, who's right on your corner, and then, when I did, he said to go home, but I came by to look at your house, only another warden told me I had to get off the street or else, so I didn't know where to go except your building, and that's when I rang your bell." I said the whole thing in one sentence like that, not exactly looking at her neither.

"How did you know I lived here?"

I stared at the picture of the air force soldier. "The . . . the other day I followed you."

"Followed me!"

"Uh-huh. . . ."

"When?"

"After you went to a house on Hicks Street."

"Hicks Street?"

"You know. . . ."

She folded her hands in her lap and studied me. There were these lines across her forehead. "Howie, that was Acting Superintendent Wolch's home. Dr. Lomister's boss."

"I know. Remember? I told you."

"Howie Crispers," Miss Gossim said, staring hard at me, "you seem to know a great deal about me and what I do." Her voice had become almost angry. "Is that true?"

I squirmed, but nodded.

"What else do you know?" she asked.

"You don't have no brother or sister."

"True. And . . . ?"

"Your father died a long time ago."

"Howie, how do you know all these things?"

"Just do," I said, not explaining that those last bits came from Denny.

"Anything else?"

That's when I gave away my big card. "Your name is Rolanda."

That made her smile. "Do you like the name?"

"Yeah. Who's that?" I suddenly asked her, pointing to the picture on the table.

She turned from me to the picture and stared at it. Then, just like this, she said, "My husband."

I looked up at her, surprised. "I didn't know you had one. He in the air force?"

"Yes."

"A pilot?"

"Yes."

"Oh, wow. . . . What's he fly?"

"P-38s."

"They're my favorite. Where's he stationed?"

All of a sudden she covered her face with her hands.

"Miss Gossim," I said, starting to get frightened. "What's the matter?"

"Howie, I don't know where he is."

"Oh," I said. Then, seeing how upset she was, I said, "You know, when my pop writes, the censors take out that sort of stuff too. We just got a Swiss-cheese letter from him. My mom thinks he's in Liverpool. Merry Old England. Only he's coming back out of convoy. See, for Easter. I don't know why. It sure ain't safe."

"Do you worry a lot about him?" she asked.

"You bet. I get all these really bad dreams. About his ship getting hit by torpedoes. With all these sharks in the water. They eat him alive. There's this blood and gore. Arms and legs go floating by. A whole head—"

"Howie! How horrible!"

"I know, but he always comes home. I bet your . . . husband is just not allowed to tell you where he is either."

"Howie," she whispered, "I . . . I don't even know if he's alive."

"You don't?"

She got all silent. Then, with a little sigh, she said, "I'm afraid for these days it's a rather common story. You see, we met last Christmastime at a servicemen's canteen. We liked each other—a lot. Really hit it off. For six days we palled around. Suddenly he got orders to report overseas. Though we didn't know each other for very long, we . . . got . . . married.

"But, Howie—I don't know why I'm telling you these things—it happened so quickly, maybe he didn't have time to inform anyone that I'm . . . his wife. Or maybe in the rush he lost my address. Except that would mean, if something happened to him, I . . . I wouldn't ever know."

I stared at her. She was holding one knee up, leaning slightly back. The top part of her bathrobe had fallen away so I could see part of her bosom. I stared.

"Then of course," she went on, not paying any attention to me, "like tonight, the sirens go on, and it's dark, and here I am, alone, thinking so much about him . . . the way you do about your father."

I swallowed hard. "Miss Gossim?"

"Yes?"

"If you're married, how come . . . how come it's still *Miss*?"

That room was pretty dim, but I could see she blushed. "Oh, well, we married . . . quickly. Not really a secret. But almost one. At Borough Hall. We agreed we'd have a real wedding. As soon as peace comes. When he comes back. . . ." Her voice went fruity as she added, "If he comes back."

"What's his name?"

"Smitty." She took a deep breath and looked around. "I'm not a very good hostess, am I? I should be offering you something. Would you like a glass of milk? A cracker? I don't have much."

"No, thanks."

She sat there, thinking I didn't know what. Then the candle sputtered out. It got darker than before. Maybe the dark made me feel, you know, bolder, 'cause I said, "I bet I know why you got fired."

"Do you?"

Like in class, I raised my hand. "Can I say?"

"Yes. . . ."

"Dr. Lomister wanted to marry you, but when he found out you were already married, he got so jealous he fired you."

She came out with one of her big laughs. But she got serious again quick. "No," she said with a sigh. "That's not what it is."

I felt stupid.

"But what made you think that?" she asked.

"Just did."

I waited for her to say something else. When she didn't, I said, "Then . . . how come you got fired?"

She sighed.

"Did your mother die?" I asked.

"No. She's living in Indiana."

"Then how come you're living here?"

"Howie Crispers, now I know why you got your name."

"Why?"

"Knock knock."

"Who's there?"

"How."

"How who?"

"How-ie Crispers."

"Don't mean nothing."

She got up and stood by the window, arms folded, and looked at the blacked-out city. "It's so dark," she said.

I felt like saying it was pretty dark inside. Instead I went and stood near her, staring out the window too. Searchlights were still sweeping the sky, looking for enemy planes. I could smell her flowerlike perfume.

"Do you think German bombers are coming?" I asked.

"We're very far from Europe," she said. "I think we're perfectly safe."

"That's what I told my kid sister."

"What's her name?"

"Gloria. She's in third grade. Mrs. Khol's class."

"Of course."

"What about spies?" I asked. "You think they're around?"

She looked at me. "You do worry a lot, don't you?"

"Sort of."

"Well," she said, "I have to admit, I worry too."

The two of us, side by side, kept staring out the window.

"Howie," she asked, "why are you so interested in me?"

I was afraid to look up. My heart was pounding. I said, "I guess . . . I like you. A lot."

She reached out and mussed my hair. "When my baby comes," she said, all quietlike, "and if it's a boy, I hope he's as sweet as you."

Slowly it began to sink in what she was getting at. "Miss Gossim," I said, still staring out the window, "are you . . . going to have . . . a kid?"

"Yes," she whispered after a moment.

"Really?"

"Really," she said, sounding very sad.

I was afraid to look at her. "Is . . . is *that* how come Lomister fired you?"

She hesitated. Then she said, "Yes."

"But why?"

"There's a rule that says teachers can't be . . . expecting and teach."

"How'd he find out?"

"Mrs. Partridge told him."

"Creepers! Why'd she do that?"

"She was trying to help me."

I thought about what Miss Gossim said for a while. Then I said, "But what are you going to do?"

"I'll go back to be with my mother."

"In Indiana?"

"Yes."

"That's so far!"

"Not really."

"In a midsized city?"

"On a farm, actually."

I looked up at her. Tears were rolling down her cheeks. Me, I was sort of dying.

"Well," she said, "I can't stay here. Not alone. Not without a job. Or money. I have very little. So I save a little every week. I hadn't planned on going back quite so soon. But now I will."

I kept studying her face. "How come you don't have more money?"

"I'm afraid teachers don't get paid much."

"They don't?"

"No. But Howie, when I go, how will Smitty ever find me? Or, if something happens to him, how will I ever know? I have no way of contacting him."

So then I said, "Maybe I could speak to my mom and you could stay with us. You could come here every day and check to see if he came."

She sort of smiled. "I don't think that would work. I think I better stick to my plan."

For a while neither of us said anything.

She turned to me. "Howie, I shouldn't be talking to you like this. But I must admit, it's good to talk to *some-one*. Except you must *promise* that you won't tell anyone about these things. Are you good at secrets?"

I held out my fist, pinky out. "I swear."

She looked at my hand. "What's that mean?"

"When you make a swear, you do pinkies."

She laughed her laugh and held out a fist, pinky out.

I did the chop.

Just as I did, the air raid siren started blaring again. The all-clear signal. The city began to blink on.

Miss Gossim gave me a little shake. "Howie, I think you better get on home. I'm sure your mother is very worried."

"Yes, miss."

"Howie!" she called after me as I headed down the hall toward the steps.

I stopped and turned.

"Remember your promise," she called.

"Cross my heart and hope to die," I said, and hurried away.

When I stepped out of the apartment onto the sidewalk, I looked up. The city lights were back. And all the stars were gone.

PART TWO

Eighth Army Artillery Smashes
Nazi Tank Waves Without Yielding.
U.S. Wounded Stick to Guns to Beat
Off German Thrusts.

Ration Points Set for Meat,
Canned Fish, Fat, Cheese.

Director of the Office of
War Information Reveals
U-boat Toll in Recent Convoys.

24

OKAY, NEXT DAY, Thursday, plenty of stuff happened.

First off, even though I walked with Denny to school, I still didn't tell him what happened the night before. He never asked. The truth was, I was keeping it to myself. I didn't want to share.

After checking headlines at Teophilo's, Denny and me talked about the war. What was going on in North Africa. Where his father was. The Pacific news. And my father, wherever he was, dodging Nazi U-boats.

In school I kept watching to see if Miss Gossim would act different to me. She didn't, except once. Sort of. It was at family news time. Gladys Halflinger announced to the class that her mother was expecting. When she did, I thought Miss Gossim took a quick look over at me. Maybe I was only wishing it.

Then, it being Thursday, we did war stamps.

War stamps went like this: The U.S. government had to buy all kinds of stuff for our soldiers. Guns, ammo, airplanes, ships, tanks. So what did they do? They borrowed money from people by getting them to buy war bonds. The thing was, they borrowed from kids too by getting us to buy war stamps.

When you bought a stamp, you pasted it in a special book. Fill your book and you'd get a twenty-five-dollar war bond. The government promised to give the money back with extra. Soon as peace came. Most of us bought only one or two stamps a week, so it took a long time to fill a book. Almost as long as it took to win the war.

You could buy stamps for ten cents or twenty-five cents. I liked the ten centers best. They were red with a picture of a minuteman on them.

Thursday, Billy Wiggins was war-stamp monitor. If you were war-stamp monitor, you stood in front of the class and made a speech about why it was a good thing to buy stamps and support our boys in the war. Then we kids would line up. As Miss Gossim watched, we'd buy stamps from the monitor. Stick them in our books.

That time, Billy made a speech about how bad Hitler was. Nothing I didn't know. Then, as the kids paid their coins, making a little pile on Miss Gossim's desk, I noticed she was looking at the money. Looking upset, actually.

Then I remembered her saying how little money she had, being a teacher and all.

I was thinking, Holy moley, how am I going to help her? I mean, she only had a couple of days left. Maybe she had a plan for her life, but I didn't. It was what the movie serials—like in *Dick Tracy Against Crime Inc.*— called "a desperate situation." If something didn't happen, there wasn't going to *be* a next week. It was gonna be "The End." Goom-bye.

But at three o'clock, all she said was "Children, study your history books tonight. Tomorrow we'll have our test on the American Revolution."

25

AFTER SCHOOL, Denny and me, we were walking home. No one was saying anything 'til he said, "Learn anything new about Miss Gossim?"

Now, remember, I hadn't told Denny nothing about my visit to Miss Gossim's. For that matter, I never told him I'd seen her looking over the cliff either. Hadn't even told him where she was living.

At first all I said was "I guess she's still only got 'til Monday."

He said, "When do you think she'll tell the class she's going?"

"The last hour, I bet."

Then he said, "You figure out yet why she got fired?"

Soon as he said that, I knew I couldn't handle it alone. I was a kid. This was supercolossal grown-up stuff. If I was going to help Miss Gossim, I needed help.

So I said, "Remember the other day when we were collecting, how I followed her?"

"Yeah?"

"Well, I found out where she lives."

"Oh, sure," he said, smooth as a Fudgsicle. "Hicks and Orange. That apartment building. Apartment Five-C."

I looked at him, really annoyed. Then I remembered that he knew about her father being dead and he hadn't told me none of that stuff either. So I said, "How come you know so much about her?"

"Because," he said.

"Because *what*?"

"Because I do," he explained.

I was about to get really mad at him and call off our no-secrets pact. Then I remembered I hadn't told him stuff either. So we were almost even. In fact, the only way to get really even was to let him know what happened to me. So I said, "Well, I know a lot more."

"Like what?"

"Hey, wise guy," I said, "how come I'm supposed to tell you stuff when you don't tell me the stuff you're supposed to tell me?"

"I dunno," he said.

But, let's face it, the best part about having a secret is telling someone. So after a while I said, "Promise not to tell?"

Right away he poked out his pinky. No two ways about it, Denny loved swears. We hooked. "No fins," I said.

"No fins," he echoed.

I chopped.

"Okay," I said, "she . . . she got fired because she's going . . . to have a baby."

He stopped dead short and stared at me, mouth open, like he was waiting for a fly to pop in. You can't believe how good I felt knowing something he didn't know.

"That really true?" he said.

I nodded.

"How come you know?"

"She told me."

"She *told* you?"

"Yeah," I said, kind of casual, the way the hero says it in movies.

"She did? When?"

So I upped and told how I visited Miss Gossim in her apartment. The more I said, the more his mouth hung open.

He said, "You saying she really, truly—no fooling or nothing—told you?"

"Swear to God."

"Oh, wow. How did she look?"

"Like a movie star."

"What . . . what was she wearing?"

"A bathrobe."

"A bathrobe! Willikers. . . ."

"Yeah," I said. "Glassy." Then I said, "Only I didn't tell you because I told her I wouldn't."

"Then how come you're telling me now?" He sounded angry.

"Don't you want to know?"

"Yeah, but . . ."

"Hey, Denny . . ."

"Hay is for horses."

"Come on, Denny, tell the truth. How much you like Miss Gossim? A *whole* lot, right?"

"I guess," he said.

"Well, can't we both like her and still be best friends?" I asked.

He thought a minute. "Suppose."

"Then you should tell me how come you knew all that stuff about her I didn't know."

So Denny said, "Remember when Lomister put me in the office for running down the hall to the bathroom when I had the runs?"

"Yeah."

"When I was sitting in there, I asked Mrs. Partridge all about Miss Gossim. She told me."

"You didn't spy or nothing?"

"Do I look like a J. Edgar Hoover?"

"You wear a bow tie."

"Doesn't mean . . ."

Then I said, "Come on, Denny, I really want to help her. Only I don't know what to do. I mean, if you were going to be . . . you know . . . expecting . . . would you know what to do?"

"Boys can't have babies."

"I know that! I'm just saying, if you could, would you?"

"No," he admitted.

"Well, then, okay. It must be scary. When she leaves, we probably ain't ever going to see her again."

"She going home to Indiana?"

"Yeah," I said, sore because that was still another thing he knew which now I knew, only he hadn't told me before.

We went on, checked the headlines at the newspaper stand, but when we got to his tailor shop, I was still sore. So all I said was "See you in the morning."

"Can't," he said. "I have to make a delivery for my mother first."

"Okay. Goom-bye."

"Hey, Howie," he called after me.

"What?"

"Plant you now, dig you later."

I trudged off, not looking back. I was thinking, What was the point of telling him all that? I still didn't know how I was going to help Miss Gossim.

26

WHEN I GOT HOME, I sat on my front stoop. The sun was shining warm enough so that windows were open. The skinny pin-oak trees in their squares of dirt had some green buds. Kids were jumping rope. Playing marbles. Hopscotch.

Not wanting to think about Miss Gossim, I started studying my American history book.

But Gloria, up in the apartment, had the radio on so loud I could hear the soap opera she was listening to:

> "Time now for *The Romance of Helen Trent*! The real-life drama of Helen Trent, who—when life mocks her, breaks her hopes, dashes her against the rocks of despair—fights back bravely, success- fully, to prove what so many long to prove in their own lives . . . that because a woman is thirty- five—"

I ran up to the apartment. "Gloria!" I screamed. "Turn the radio off! I'm trying to study!"

All she did was make it lower.

Being already upstairs, I sat in the kitchen and kept reading. After a while Gloria came into the room.

"What you studying?"

"The Revolution."

"What's that?" she asked.

"Go read *Orphan Annie*."

She stood behind me, reading my book over my shoulder. "What's a pet-i-tion?" she said, pointing to the word in my book. She was a good reader.

Naturally, I had to show off like the big brother I was. "A petition is what people do when they don't like something. See, they write up a sort of letter saying that they don't want something to happen. Everyone signs it. Then the people who are doing the thing they don't want them to do read the petition and change their minds because they see people don't like what they're doing. That's a petition. In case you didn't know, the Declaration of Independence was sort of a petition."

She thought for a moment and then said, "What's the Declaration of Independence?"

I said, "Go ask Helen Trent."

"Sad Sam," she called me as she walked away.

The thing was, after she went, I started thinking about what I'd just been saying. And I began to have this idea: What about doing a petition about Miss Gossim? I'd get everyone in class to sign it, then give it to Dr. Lomister. That would make him un-fire Miss Gossim.

The more I sat there thinking about it, the more I liked it. I got so excited, I got out some paper and a pencil.

It took a while, with bunches of cross outs, but what I did finally read like this:

Dr. Lomister!
We hold the truth to be self evidence! Class Five-B wants
Miss Gossim not to be fired because she is expecting! She
is a good teacher! She is married and her husband is in the
Air Force. So she does not know even where he is! So she
should stay!

The exclamation points were so Lomister would know we really meant it.

Then I signed it, big, like John Hancock.

I figured I'd bring it to school next day. Get the

whole class to sign it.

I have to admit, though, I did remember my promise to Miss Gossim that I wasn't going to do anything. But I was telling myself I *had* to do something. See, I couldn't do nothing for my pop, or Denny's dad, but I could do something for Miss Gossim. I mean, Pop was somewhere. Denny's father was in Africa. She was close. Understand? Doing *something* was better than doing nothing. "Hey," I said, giving myself permission, "don't you know there's a war on?"

Rommel Hangs On in North Africa.
Heavy U.S. Casualties Will
Mark Victory.

Meat Shops Bare All over City.
No Relief in Sight.

Center of Berlin Blasted in
Heaviest Raid.

27

OKAY. Next morning, petition in my hand, I set off to school early.

I brought along a fountain pen (my father's good one, which I wasn't supposed to take) so kids could put their names to it. All the same, I was worried nobody would sign. Nervous about Miss Gossim too. What if she found out what I was doing? I'd be in for it. Except I didn't know what else to do. So there I was, doing it.

By the time I reached the school yard, some kids were already there, talking, fooling around. I checked for kids from my class. The first one I saw was Gladiola Alvarez. She was sitting on the ground, her back against a wall.

"Hey, Gladiola!" I called, running toward her. "I gotta talk to you."

Gladiola was this small dark-skinned girl who had come from Puerto Rico. She had these two brothers. One was in the navy, the other the army. Her father worked in a factory. I never heard her talk about her mother. Her clothes were always poor looking but clean. In class she was pretty quiet except during math, which she was good at.

"You talking to me?" she said, pointing to herself. I mean, we weren't close friends. She lived over in the State Street projects, where I never went.

"It's about Miss Gossim," I said.

"Yeah, what?"

I told her everything.

The more I said, the more serious Gladiola looked.

"You saying she's getting fired because she's having a baby?" she said when I was done.

"Yeah."

"Who's the father?"

"Her husband. Name is Smitty. He's in the air force. Only she doesn't know where."

"She really marry him?"

Surprised, I said, "You saying she didn't?"

Gladiola shook her hand like it had been burned. "Ooooo, man," she said. "That Miss Gossim is into some big troubles."

"That's why I made up this petition," I said, showing it to her.

"A petition for what?"

"To help her." I gave it to her.

"Yeah," she said after reading it. "That's nice. But what am I supposed to do about it?"

"Sign it," I said. I held up my pop's pen.

She took the pen but held back, looking at me, suspicious. "If I sign, you saying she can stay?"

"I'm just saying if we get the whole class to sign it, she will."

"I do it," she asked, "am I going to get in any trouble or anything?"

"Naw," I said. "See, I already signed it. And like it says in the history book, it's a free country. We can talk what we want. It's what the war's about."

"Howie, this ain't talking."

"Come on, Gladiola, you want to help Miss Gossim, or don't you?"

"Yeah, she's a nice lady," she said, and signed the petition, then handed it back to me. "Hope it works, man."

"The only thing is," I warned her, "you can't tell her what we're doing. It's a top war secret."

"Don't worry. Nobody talks to me anyway. First time you talking to me, right?"

By the time the first bell rang, I had—besides my own—seven more kids' signatures. Only problem was—even though I asked people not to talk—the news about Miss Gossim in the petition was spreading fast.

I didn't get a chance to speak to Denny till we were in class. Then, just when I was about to tell him, Miss Gossim said, "All right children, let's get started. I think Betty Wu is flag monitor this morning. Betty, please come up and lead us in the Pledge of Allegiance."

I got to Denny during snack time. When I told him what I was doing, he thought it was a great idea. Said he'd help too. Between us, we figured we'd get the rest of the class during lunchtime. We almost did too. Except by then the whole class knew what was going on. They were coming to us to sign.

So far, so good. But what happened next was this: It was almost the end of lunch period. We were out in the school yard. Denny and I were just getting Horace Ducada to sign, when the lineup bell rings.

What you have to understand about this Horace Ducada is this. He was one of those kids who always did what adults told him to do. I mean, right away. No matter who or what. He just did. *Bang!* You'd tell him to do something, he did it. The kid should have been a windup toy. And see, the school bell meant *get moving*. So what did Horace do? He stuffed the petition into his pocket and marched off.

"Hey, Horace," I yelled. "Give it back!"

"The bell rang," he said.

"Horace!"

Next second the second bell went for the end of lunch period. That meant, as we went back to class, Horace had the petition in his pocket.

28

SOON AS WE got back to the classroom, Miss Gossim said, "Hurry up now, children. We've a great deal to do this afternoon. No dillydallying."

The only thing was, Horace *still* had the petition. But what did he do? He went right to his seat.

I had to get the petition back. Fast. Looking round at him from my seat, I made angry wiggles with my fingers. They must have been really angry 'cause this time Horace started to pass the paper on to me—kid to kid.

And then, Betty Wu got it. Problem was, she didn't know how to be sneaky. So next thing, *bingo-be-bop!* Miss Gossim saw it.

"Betty Wu," Miss Gossim called, "is that a *note* you are passing?"

Now, maybe some other kid would have ditched the paper. Not Betty Wu. Too much the Goody Two-Shoes. She just sat there and hung her head. Like she was in some Greta Garbo movie called *Guilty*. Even worse, the next moment she lifted her hand up. She was holding the petition.

"Yes, Miss Gossim," she whispered. "I beg you to forgive me. I have done a bad thing."

I was jumping out of my skin. Remember how I told you how Miss Gossim had this strict rule about not passing notes? Whenever she caught anyone doing it, she read the whole note out loud to the class.

So, sure as the red stop light comes after the green, Miss Gossim said, "Now, Betty, you know the rules we have about note passing. All passed notes must be read out loud so that everyone may know what's been said. We don't want to have secrets in class, do we? Please bring that note to me."

Betty brought her the petition.

Miss Gossim held it up. "Is this your note, Betty?" she asked.

Betty shook her head.

"I see. Were you just passing it on for someone?"

Betty nodded.

"Do you know whose note it is?"

"Yes, Miss Gossim."

"Whose?"

Betty looked at her patent-leather shoes, which were shiny enough she could have counted chewing-gum wads on the bottoms of desks.

"Betty, I really need to know," Miss Gossim said.

After a moment Betty said, "It belongs to Howie."

"Howie?" Miss Gossim said, and looked around at me. "Howie, is this your note?"

"Sort of," I said, cracking my knuckles.

The whole class was seat squirming. They knew what was going to happen. And me, I was starting to slide under my desk like the *Titanic* went down after it hit that iceberg.

Didn't matter. Miss Gossim unfolded the petition

and started to read it out loud:

> "Dr. Lomister!
> We hold the truth to be self evidence! Class Five-B wants
> Miss Gossim not to be fired because she is—"

Suddenly she stopped reading out loud. I mean, *stopped*. You could hear the brakes. The petition in her hand made this small rustling sound. A kind of shaking.

I could see her eyes reading the rest of it. Including the names, which was everybody in the class. Then, after a while, she slowly lowered the paper. Let me tell you, her face was *red*. She was breathing hard too. And the muscles round her neck were jive dancing.

None of us said nothing. We just sat there, staring at her. Sort of like waiting for the next bomb to drop.

"Howie Crispers," she finally said, "is this your . . . doing?"

I couldn't say nothing.

"Is it?" she asked again with a whole lot of teacher in her voice.

"Yes, Miss Gossim," I said.

"Why?"

"You know, like the Declaration of Independence."

I never saw Miss Gossim's eyes angry like the way they got then. But then—*whoosh!*—all that anger melted like toasted cheese on burnt toast. What came next was a lot worse: tears.

"Howie," she got out in a busted voice, "I'm . . . *very* disappointed in you."

It felt like my heart was in my feet and leaking over the floor. Let me tell you, it would have taken a blotter to soak me up.

Miss Gossim wiped away some tears, closed her eyes, then opened them again, and made herself a smile. All lip. No teeth.

"Well," she said, "I guess you children know all about me and my . . . life. Yes, I am going to have a child. Which I think . . . is a wonderful thing. But . . . yes, because of that, I have been asked to leave. My last day with you will be next Monday."

There was this low kind of moan from the kids.

Susan Pollador raised her hand.

"Yes, Susan."

Susan said, "Do you have to?"

Miss Gossim took a deep breath. "I wish it weren't so. But it is." She looked around the room at us. She could have been the bearded lady in the circus the way we were staring at her.

"Actually, I shouldn't be angry," she said. "I'm touched that you all care so much. And I do love you. Each and every one of you."

She took another deep breath. "Howie, may I ask, what were you going to do with your . . . declaration?"

"Give it to Dr. Lomister," I got out like a frog with a sore throat.

"I see. Class, to tell you the truth, I don't think this petition would be very helpful. In the world there are many rules—good ones as well as those we don't like. But in a civilized country we must follow them or try to change them democratically. That's the way our nation works. I know you all want to help. And I truly thank you. But it's not possible." She folded up the petition and put it on her desk.

"Howie," she said, "you had best stay after school so we can talk."

"Yes, Miss Gossim."

The room was like an empty haunted house. No sound.

No breathing. Even the ghost had taken a powder. Miss Gossim didn't seem to know what to do. Then, softly, she said, "Now, class, we are going to turn to our grammar lesson. Is there anyone who can tell me what an adjective is?"

29

FIVE MINUTES AFTER three. Up in Classroom Five-B there wasn't nobody but me and Miss Gossim. She was sitting at her desk doing papers, with the petition off to one side. I was sitting at my desk, hands folded, feet together. Now and again I pulled a thread on my red tie. Fiddled with my dog tag. Cracked my knuckles. Meanwhile, George Washington, Abraham Lincoln, and President Roosevelt were all staring at me. They didn't look too happy.

Miss Gossim worked for about half an hour. I listened to the pencil scratches. Once and a while she lifted her head. Maybe she looked at me. Only it was as if I wasn't there. I mean, she didn't say or do anything.

About three-thirty she put aside her papers. Folded her hands. Just stared at me. That time—I could tell—she *was* seeing me. She didn't look mad. Just, sad.

She gave off this sigh, reached for the petition, unfolded it, maybe read it through—I don't know. Put it back on her desk.

"Well, Howie," she finally said, "do you want to tell me about this?"

I was staring into the bottom of my inkwell. Wishing I could hide there.

"I want to believe you were trying to help me," she said.

"I was," I said, squirming in my seat.

"Howie, do you remember when I told you about . . . my life, you promised you wouldn't tell anyone?"

"Sort of."

"We even hooked pinkies. Remember?"

"Yeah, but . . ."

"But what?"

"I wanted to . . ."

"To what?"

"Help you."

Her smile muscles tightened. "I see," she said. "But

now, because of you, *everybody* knows about my private life. That's not what I wanted. I'm a grown-up, Howie. I can take care of myself."

"Don't grown-ups need kids—sometimes?" I tried.

She sighed. "I suppose they do."

"Can't this be one of the times?"

"I don't think so."

"Miss Gossim," I said, "I didn't mean nothing bad."

"I'm sure you didn't."

The room turned into this zeppelin of silence.

I lifted my head. "Miss Gossim . . ."

"Yes, Howie."

"Can I say something?"

"You may."

"I just don't think it's fair, you being fired, that's all."

She looked at me for this long while. I could see tears in her eyes. "Well, Howie, I don't think it's fair either. But I'm afraid there's not much I can do about it. It's simply the way things are. I have to manage as best I can. And I will."

"But . . . but," I cried out, "what's going to happen to you?"

"I'll go back home."

"To *Indiana*?" I said.

She smiled. "It's a lovely place."

"But you don't have no money!"

"Howie, please, I can handle my own life."

I felt like crying. "Will I ever see you again?"

"I don't know. I hope so."

I was looking at my hands, afraid to look at her, as if maybe—*poof!*—she suddenly would be gone.

"Oh, Howie," she pleaded. "This is something I have to deal with alone. I'm the adult concerned. You're only a child. In times to come, you'll be able to deal with these problems. And you'll do it well. You're going to be a fine young man. But . . . not yet."

"Miss Gossim?" I said.

"Yes?"

"Don't you know there's a war on?"

She gave off another sigh and picked up the petition. "Howie, please do *not* give this to Dr. Lomister. He promised to write nice things about me so I can get another job. Indiana, perhaps. Or here in Brooklyn. Howie, I can't afford to anger him. Please, please, don't try to help me anymore."

"Okay," I managed.

"Now," she went on, holding out the petition. "Take this back. I'd rather you threw it away."

Completely miserable, I got to my feet, came forward, and took the paper.

"Howie," she said softly, touching my arm, "thank you for trying to be helpful. Now, I will see you on Monday. Remember to study for your math test. And Howie . . ."

"Yes, Miss Gossim."

"Let's make Monday—my last day—a good one."

"Yes, Miss Gossim."

"I know how we can make it really good."

"How?"

"If you get a hundred percent on your math test."

I sighed. "I don't think I can."

"Hey," she said with a smile that hurt my heart, "don't you know there's a war on?"

Afraid to look back, I stuffed the petition into my pocket, took up my books, and got out of the room as fast as I could go.

30

DENNY WAS WAITING for me on the school steps.

"What happened?" he asked.

I didn't want to talk. But Denny pushed. "You going to tell me?"

"About what?"

"Who do you think? Miss Gossim."

I gave him a look. The guy was my bestest friend. And he was upset like everyone else. So what could I do? I told him what happened in the classroom, that's what.

"Where's the petition?" he said.

"My pocket. She gave it back to me. Made me promise I wouldn't give it to Lomister."

"That stinks," he said. "My old man is in North Africa, but she can't have a kid."

We headed up Hicks Street toward home, stopping only to check headlines.

"Going to the movies tomorrow?" I asked after a while. "Chapter Seven of *Junior G-Men of the Air*."

"I s'pose. . . ."

We went on some more. Then he said, "Hear anything from your dad?"

"Yeah. He's coming home. Be back home by Easter."

"Lucky stiff."

"All he has to do is get by the U-boat wolf packs."

"He will."

"He's traveling out of convoy."

Denny didn't say nothing to that. So I said, "What's with your pop?"

"The Allies are closing in. It's a pincer movement. They'll get Rommel soon. When they finally get him, my dad'll write. A lot."

I looked at him. I was wondering if he really believed that. Because all of a sudden, the whole world seemed scary. I mean, what would happen if his dad got killed? Or if my pop did? Of if my mom didn't put in a rivet right? And what about Miss Gossim's husband? Or her? And holy smoke, what was going to happen to me?

"Hey, Denny," I said.

"What?"

"It's okay you didn't tell me that stuff you knew about Miss Gossim. I mean, we're still best friends, right?"

"Sure," he said. But after another block he stopped. "There's one other thing I never told you."

"What?"

"It's Miss Gossim's first name. It's Rolanda. Bet you didn't know that. Since we're best friends, I thought you'd want to know."

I looked at him. "Thanks," I said. "It's a good name."

We stopped in front of his store. "I got to make some deliveries," he said. "See you at the movies tomorrow."

"Okay," I said, feeling like the one and only sad sack. "See you."

31

WHEN I GOT HOME, Gloria was sitting on our front stoop with her girlfriend, Heddy. They were working on their paper-doll collection, trying on different costumes. You know, sometimes fancy dance dresses, sometimes WAC uniforms. "Where you been?" she asked, not even looking up.

"I was kept after school," I let slip.

She lifted her face for that. "Ooooo! Mom's going to be mad at you. How come?"

"None of your beeswax."

She stuck her tongue out at me.

I went up to the apartment. In the kitchen I drank a glass of Ovaltine. Then I read through the petition a few times. I kept thinking how good it was. What a low-down dirty rotten shame we couldn't give it to Lomister. But I had promised. I couldn't get Miss Gossim mad at me again. Not on her last day.

Feeling bad, I went to my bedroom. Out from under my bed I dragged my orange-crate boxes. One was for my comic-book collection. The other had all my toys. I took out this model airplane I'd made. A P-38. My favorite fighter. Smitty's plane.

Lying on my bed, I put the plane through maneuvers. Complete with sound effects. I was thinking, I'm Smitty, and I'm strafing Lomister. I'm hitting him so hard he was begging for help. Him and his rules!

Doing that war stuff got me thinking about my pop again, wondering where he was. Somewhere in the middle of the Atlantic Ocean. That got me to wishing all over again that he wasn't traveling out of convoy. Gave me the willies whenever I thought about it. What was the point of his coming back for Easter if he was only going to get himself sunk dead?

Next second I was seeing all these Nazi wolf-pack submarines prowling the ocean. Waiting for him. I even saw a torpedo slicing through the water like an angry shark. Nothing but teeth. I scared myself so bad I put the model away.

Back in the kitchen I listened to my favorite radio shows. First, *Jack Armstrong*, then *Superman*, finally *Sky King*. Least, in those shows, everything worked out okay.

I was halfway through *Sky King*. Sky and Penny, who were the characters on the show, had just trapped this Japanese spy (who had a huge bomb) in the boiler room of a cannon factory, when my sister came in. Her friend Heddy had gone home.

She stood by the door, staring at me.

"What you looking at?" I asked her.

"You."

"Why?"

"You look sick," she said.

I sighed. "I am sick."

"What kind of sick?"

"Sick in the head."

"How come?"

So I said, "You'd be sick if your favorite teacher got fired."

"Miss Gossim got fired?"

"Yup."

I got up and stormed down to my room, slamming the door behind me. Then I flung myself on my bed and pushed my face into the pillow.

There was a knock on the door. I didn't answer. Another knock.

"What do you want?"

"Talk to you."

"Go away!"

"Don't have to."

"Why?"

"It's my room too."

"Find your own room."

"Can't."

"Why?"

"There's a housing shortage."

Gloria opened the door and sat down across the way

from me on her bed. After a while she said, "Tell me about Miss Gossim."

"Don't want to."

"Please."

"Why should I?"

"I'm your sister."

"So what?"

"Because if Pop got killed and if Mom died, I'd be your whole family. Then I'd *have* to know all your secrets. That's what a family is, related secrets."

"That's just soap operas."

"Howie," she screamed, "tell me!"

Well the thing is, I told her. Not about the dumb-waiter and sneaking into the house, just about Lomister going to Mrs. Wolch. And I didn't say nothing about going to Miss Gossim's apartment either. Just what was happening to her. As I was talking, Gloria just sat there, staring at me, not saying a word.

When I was done, I said, "Anyway, that's why I feel sick."

At first she didn't say nothing. Then she said, "Howie . . ."

"What?"

"In soap operas they always figure out how to do things."

"Go take a flying hike."

She sniffed. "Well, if I were you, I know just what I'd do."

I couldn't believe it. There she was: She just heard the whole thing. Right off, she's telling me what to do. I didn't say nothing. I just lay there, really annoyed.

"Don't you want to know what to do?" she asked.

"No."

"You just don't want to know because I'm your kid sister."

"Buzz off."

"But I figured it all out."

"Did not."

"I did!"

"Okay, smarty-pants, what?"

"If I'm smart," she pouted, "it's because I'm like a smart sandwich. You and Mom are the bread. I'm the in-between."

"That's so stupid."

"It's true!"

"Prove it."

"You told Miss Gossim you wouldn't give that petition

to Dr. Lomister. Right?"

I rolled over, my back to her. "Right."

"And people should always keep their promise. But did she tell you anything about Lomister's *boss*?"

"Boss?"

"You know, that Mrs. Wolch you were talking about."

"What about her?"

"Howie, in the soap operas people always go behind other people's backs. So if Dr. Lomister went behind Miss Gossim's back to that lady and said she should fire Miss Gossim, then you should go behind his back to that same lady and ask her to keep Miss Gossim. You know, give that lady that petition."

I let her idea sink in. The more it sank, the better I liked it. I swung around to face Gloria. "But Monday's Miss Gossim's last day."

"Then you better go see that Mrs. Wolch right away."

I shook my head. "I couldn't do it. I'd be too scared. Anyway, with petitions, it only works if you get tons of people."

"Get the kids from your class to go with you," she said.

"Great! I don't even know where they live, mostly."

Neither of us said anything for a bit. But that's when I

had *my* idea. "Hey," I cried, "the kids' movie tomorrow morning. My whole class goes. I could get them to go after that."

"See," she said, and made a fist. "We can do it."

"All right, here's my plan," I said. "I'll go to the movies, and get the kids—lots of them—and bring them to Mrs. Wolch's house. What do you think?"

"Ta-da-de-da-taaaa!"

"What's that mean?"

"On soap operas, when something important happens, they do organ music."

"Only one thing," I added.

"What?"

"Don't tell Mom."

"How come?"

"She's got enough to worry about."

Gloria gave me a look. "Maybe, maybe not."

32

I STARTED MAKING DINNER. Wasn't much. A can of

spaghetti with sauce. Except I put some chunks of Spam in it to make it better.

My mom got home. First thing, she looked at the kitchen table, checking for a letter from my pop. Only there wasn't any.

"Maybe," I said, "he's almost home."

She gave me a sad face, but all she said was "Sorry I'm late. How you kids doing?" She was tired.

"You know what happened?" Gloria said right off. "Howie had to stay in after school."

I shot my sister this dirty look. First she wants to be my friend, then she tries to turn me in. A stool pigeon.

"Howard Bellington Crispers," my mom said, "what happened now?"

"Can I tell you after dinner?"

"Be a pleasure," she said, which proved she was pretty worn-out.

Gloria served us dinner. While Mom ate, she showed us an alarm clock the Navy Yard gave out to all the workers.

"Why'd they do that?" I asked.

"They're supposed to help people get up and to work on time. It'll boost production."

"You're never late," Gloria said.

"Some people are."

She looked so sad we just stared at her, knowing something big was bothering her. Sure enough, after a moment she told us about this rumor going around the Yard. A huge ship convoy trying to reach England had been really cut up by the U-boats.

She didn't have to say any more. We knew she was really worried about Pop. Fact, she didn't even want to finish her dinner, not until Gloria said, the way my mom always said when we didn't eat, "Think about the poor starving children in Europe."

She ate.

33

WHILE MOM TOOK A BATH, Gloria and I cleaned up.

Then, a little later, Mom called me into her room. It was the smallest room in the apartment. Smaller even than the one Gloria and I shared. Just a bed, an old dresser, a side table. On the table was this picture she and my dad took when they got married. They were kissing.

Next to that was her new alarm clock.

"Now," she said, already in her pajamas, "what happened to you at school?"

"Aw, Ma, do I have to—"

"Howie, you don't know how tired I am. Just tell me. I need to know."

"Why?"

"Because I'm your parent, that's why. The only one around."

"Pop will be home soon. I can wait and tell him."

"Howie, just let me hear it. It'll be a relief to worry about something stupid."

"It ain't stupid."

"Try me."

So, like I always do, I told. The whole kit and caboodle. About Miss Gossim, her expecting, about her being fired. Except I have to admit, like with Gloria, I didn't tell her *how* I found out. You know, the dumbwaiter. Nothing neither about my visit to Miss Gossim's apartment. But I did tell her about the petition, how I got caught, which is why I had to stay in after school. And, I admit, I also didn't tell her what I was going to do with the petition. I figured, it hadn't happened, so no point in confessing yet. I could do that later.

It was a good thing she was so tired. She smiled at some of what I said. Looked sad at other times. Mostly she wasn't angry or nothing.

"I did have one other idea," I added.

"What?"

"Maybe Miss Gossim could stay with us."

"Your teacher? *Here*?"

"Sure. Gloria and I could take care of her baby in our room. She could share with you. With the housing shortage tons of people share."

Mom sort of smiled. "Howie, we're so crowded. And what'll happen when your father gets home? We don't have room."

I almost said, But what if he doesn't come home? But I didn't.

Then she said, "Howie, it's nice you care. But didn't she say she needed to take care of herself?"

"Yeah."

"Sweetheart, she's a grown woman. She'll manage. Sometimes you have to let things happen. Okay?"

"Was I stupid?"

"No. I like it you tried to help her." She gave me a good-night kiss.

I started for the door. Then I stopped. "Mom," I said, "I'm worried about Pop."

She said, "Me too."

"Can't we get him to stay over there, wait for a convoy?"

"Howie," she said, "see that picture of your father?"

"Yeah."

"It's the first thing I look at in the morning, the last thing at night. Not much else I can do."

Her voice got teary. I came back to hug her.

When I did, she said, "You're a good kid."

"If I'm so good, can I go to the kids' movie show in the morning?"

She sighed. "You pass your math test this week?"

"A D-minus."

"That passing?"

"Yeah."

"Sure. You can go if you take Gloria with you."

"Aw, Ma, do I have to?"

"Howie," she said. "I got to work overtime tomorrow. I don't want her here alone all day."

"Ma . . ."

"Howie, don't you know there's—"

"Okay, okay!"

She fished out two quarters from her purse. Enough for two movie tickets. "And one more thing."

"What?"

"Comb your head. It's sticking up."

In our room Gloria was in bed, reading a Nancy Drew book.

"Hey, blabbermouth," I said, "you want to go to the kids' movie in the morning?"

She sat up. "Can I?"

"If you go with me."

"Sure.

"Can I go with you to that Mrs. Wolch too?"

"Just keep your mouth shut."

"I promise."

I washed up. In bed I tried to read my Big Little Book, which was *Don Winslow of the Navy*. But I couldn't think about what I was reading. I turned the lights out.

"Howie?" my sister called across in a whisper.

"What?"

"Is Pop going to be all right?"

"Oh, sure. Piece of cake."

"What kind of cake?"

"Chocolate."

"How many layers?"

"Four."

"What's between the layers?"

"More chocolate."

"Anything else?"

"There's a cherry on top."

"Okay."

She sighed, and pretty soon I could tell from her breathing she was asleep. That's the way it was with little kids.

But as I lay there in the dark, I kept thinking about the rumor Mom told us, that big convoy being hit. That and Pop.

It was all so scary, I tried to think of Miss Gossim. But all I could think of was how, after one more school day, she could be gone. For good.

PART THREE

U-boat Lair Raided.
British Bombers Drop
1,000 Tons of Bombs on
French Port.

New Ships Ready to Fight U-boats.

Eight Butchers Jailed. Get Federal
Terms for Black Market Dealing.

Stores Foraging for Long
Island Potatoes.

34

WHEN I WOKE UP, my mother had already gone to work. It was drizzling too.

On the kitchen table was this note.

Kids. Enjoy your day. I'll be home for dinner.
Keep dry. Get something at the store.

Howie, try not to worry.

> *XXX 000*
> *Mom*

She left a dollar bill and our ration book.

During breakfast, I read the back of the corn flakes box. It had these German airplane silhouettes for Junior Spotters to learn. I studied them hard. You never knew when you'd need information like that.

Then I woke Gloria. I was hoping she wouldn't want to go to the movies. Soon as she opened her eyes, I told her it was raining.

Only she said, "I don't care. I'm coming with you."

The Victory Movie Palace was over on Clark Street, a block from Hicks. Gloria and I got there half an hour before the movie began, which was nine o'clock. Even so, there was this huge line of kids waiting to get in. Some were in raincoats and galoshes. A couple had umbrellas. The rest were just getting wet like me and Gloria.

Walking to the end of the line, I saw tons of kids from school. Denny too. Soon as he saw me, he left his place and went to the back of the line with us.

"I got a great idea," I said to him right away.

"It was my idea," my sister piped in.

I knew she was going to be a nuisance. So I just ignored her and told Denny that we were going to give the petition right to Mrs. Wolch.

"Mrs. Wolch?" Denny said. "That the lady whose house you went into?"

"Right. See, if a whole bunch of us gave her the petition, she'd see we meant it. And she's Lomister's boss. So she could un-fire Miss Gossim. There must be at least ten kids from our class on line."

Denny looked at me with those big behind-the-glasses

eyes and said, "Neat-o. When we going to do it?"

"After the show."

Then my sister said, "It really was my idea."

Denny said, "And Santa Claus joined the navy."

"It's true!" my sister cried.

Denny looked at me.

"It was," I admitted. "I got the petition here." I patted my pocket.

But before we could do anything else, the doors to the movie theater opened up. There was a whoop and holler from the kids, and the line surged forward like bobby-soxers at the Paramount.

35

THAT VICTORY THEATER was big. Even so, every Saturday morning it was stuffed with kids. They were all over the place, talking, yelling, shouting, running up and down the aisles, throwing stuff—paper airplanes, candy wrappers, popcorn, spitballs—across the theater and down from the balcony, where older kids went to neck. That morning, with so many people wet from rain, it was pretty stinko too.

There was one old lady in charge. The matron, we called her. She wore a white coat like an evil doctor in a bad movie. She kept rushing around, yelling at kids, promising to kick us out if were bad. Didn't make no difference. No one stopped doing nothing. But no one got kicked out neither. Every week, same thing.

Being at the back of the line, by the time we got in the only seats we could find were in the first row. Right up front. Soon as we sat down, Denny stood up, his back to the screen. "I have to find the others," he said.

Except right about then the lights went down. That brought this huge cheer from the crowd. But Denny kept standing, facing the audience. "Down in front! Down in front!" kids screamed at him. He didn't budge.

The show started the way it always did—six cartoons, one after the other. Bugs Bunny. Donald Duck. Elmer Fudd. Tom and Jerry. Mickey Mouse. And my favorite, Mighty Mouse. The cartoons were mostly animals chasing animals, bopping each other on their heads. And at the same time all this loud, jazzy music going *Boop! Plunk! Tweet! Bang!* A regular riot. Sitting in the first row, it was like taking a bath in color and music.

Behind us kids were yelling and screaming with each film. Don't matter what it was. Or what was happening. A barrage of noise. Kids would even make paper wads and throw them up into the movie light so they glowed. You know, inside shooting stars.

Oh, sure, the matron tried to keep things quiet. But no one paid any attention to her.

I don't think Denny watched one cartoon. He kept searching the audience. Every time he spotted some kid from our class, he went to them.

"Excuse me, excuse me," he'd say as he pushed his way along the rows to shouts of "Down in front! Down in front!"

When he reached one of the kids from our class, he'd say, "You gotta meet us after the show out front. It's about Miss Gossim. We found a way to help her."

The audience didn't calm down until the *March of Time* newsreel. Then everybody got super still. Even Denny sat and watched. See, it was all about the war. Tons of moving pictures of men marching, tanks shooting, bombs dropping down from bomb bays, ships plowing through heavy seas, Germans and Japanese (hands over heads) surrendering, WACs smiling, women building ships, women pilots of the Ferry Command.

It all came with this huge voice saying how brave and determined the Free World Allies were, that it was only a matter of time before our troops would be marching home and real peace and democracy would come to the whole world. *"Time,"* the voice cried out at the end, *"marches on!"*

I'm telling you, it was really thrilling. We cheered at the end of it. And meant it too. Hey, they were our dads, moms, uncles, brothers, sisters, aunts, and cousins—our family.

After the news came the western, which brought more cheers from the audience. Finally, after the western they showed a serial chapter. My favorite part of the whole show. Chapter Seven of *Junior G-Men of the Air.*

It began with last week's ending: Lionel Croft— supposed to be sixteen years old—was flying into a Nazi ambush behind the clouds in his special biplane when his motor conked out. Except that morning they added this bit where Lionel—at the last moment—*saw* he was in a trap. So, natch, he leaped out of his plane and parachuted to safety. But, double natch, the Nazis go after him. Didn't matter. He got away, though it wasn't easy. In fact, triple natch, he was speeding away in his sporty runabout—top down—to save his girlfriend—Betty—when the wooden bridge he was on—booby-trapped by spies—exploded. Which was, quadruple natch, the end of the chapter. You didn't know if Lionel Croft was alive or not. I mean, this time it looked really bad.

But that's when the lights went on. Everybody cheered and swarmed out. If you moved fast, the theater gave you a peppermint patty when you went out to the street, where the rest of the world was still going on.

36

"STAY RIGHT HERE," Denny said to me and Gloria when we got outside. "I'll get the other kids."

In all the excitement with the movies—almost four hours' worth—I forgot we were going to Mrs. Wolch with the petition.

Denny got five kids from our class. There was Billy Wiggins, Susan Pollador, Albert Porter, Gladys Halflinger, and Toby Robinson. So with me, Denny, and my kid sister, that was eight. A few more wanted to come but couldn't.

We met on the corner of Clark and Henry streets. It had stopped raining.

To begin, Denny said, "Remember the petition we were going to give to Lomister for Miss Gossim?"

"About Miss Gossim and her baby?" Susan Pollador asked.

"Yeah."

"And being fired?" Toby Robinson said.

"Well," Denny explained, "Miss Gossim didn't want us to give it to Dr. Lomister. Okay, fine. Howie here came up with the idea of giving it to Lomister's boss."

"Who's she?" Albert Porter suddenly said, pointing at Gloria.

"My sister."

"This whole idea was mine," Gloria said.

"The thing is," I told my classmates, "the lady we have to talk to, her name is Mrs. Wolch. She's sort of like the president of all the schools in Brooklyn. Over Lomister too. So she can do whatever she wants. If we give the petition to her, she can make sure Miss Gossim stays." I held the petition up as a reminder.

"And we know where she lives," Denny put in.

"Where?"

"Right over on Hicks Street."

"Come on!"

All eight of us took off down the block, running hard. I was up front. As I was going, I stuffed the petition into my back pocket.

37

WE GOT TO Mrs. Wolch's brownstone house in nothing flat. Standing on the sidewalk, we just looked at the place. The house looked pretty big. No one said nothing.

Then Gladys Halflinger whispered, "This lady we're going to, she live in the *whole* house?"

"Just the top floor, I think," I told her.

"You sure she's even gonna be there?" Billy Wiggins wanted to know.

It was Albert Porter, after a minute, who said, "How about ringing the bell?"

Denny said, "I think Howie has a better idea."

Everybody looked at me.

I said, "The dumbwaiter. It'll take us right to her door."

"*The dumbwaiter!*" Billy Wiggins said. "You crazy or something?"

"Did it before."

"Yeah? When?"

"Last Monday."

"You really did that?" Susan Pollador asked me.

"Yeah."

"You never told me *that*," my sister said.

"Snaky," Toby Robinson said, giving me a look like I was half-crazy, half-Superman.

I had been checking where the steel door and the coal chute were. The door was closed, but like before, no lock, which meant it could be opened.

"See," I said. "You go down the coal chute, then get right to her floor. She wouldn't even see us till we got there."

"Which means," Denny added, "she won't be able to tell us to leave before we present the petition."

"No way," Susan Pollador said, backing away. "I'm not

supposed to go into other people's house. Not when I don't know them. Not down no coal chute."

"You're not supposed to either," my sister said to me.

So that's when I said, "Look, we going to help Miss Gossim, or what?" Without waiting for an answer, I went over the low fence and pulled up the steel door that covered the coal chute. "Come on! Now or never."

"Howie," my sister called, "Mom's not going to like you doing this."

"Go suck a lemon," I told her.

"Let's get moving," Denny said. He was holding up the steel door.

Susan Pollador went home. The rest stayed. So we were seven now, if you included my sister, which I didn't want to, but there wasn't no choice. Fact, she was the first to sit on the chute edge and push off. She slipped right down into the basement, nothing flat.

Then—one after the other—Billy Wiggins, Albert Porter, Gladys Halflinger, Toby Robinson, and me went down. Last to come was Denny.

38

SO THERE WE were, in the basement of Mrs. Wolch's house. Like before, it was pretty dim. But with the steel door open, we could see a lot better than when I was there before.

"Spooky down here," Albert Porter said, looking around.

"Filthy," Gloria said.

"You really did this before?" Billy Wiggins asked me.

"Yeah," I said. "Here's the dumbwaiter I went up in." I pulled the door open. They looked at it.

"Pretty small," Albert Porter said.

"We'll go one at a time," Denny suggested.

"Ain't there any steps?" Toby Robinson said.

"Back there," I said. "Only it's locked."

"What are you, some kind of snitch thief or something?" my sister said to me.

"Shut up!"

"Who's going first?" Toby Robinson asked.

I said, "Hey, I'll go. I know the way. If everybody pulls the ropes, it should go pretty fast."

"I'll go last," Denny said.

I crawled into the box, pulled in my hands and knees. Next thing, Gladys Halfinger and Billy Wiggins grabbed hold of the ropes and started pulling.

Compared to when I did it before with just myself, I went up like a Flash Gordon rocket. Only since they didn't know how far to go, I smashed into the top with this big noise.

I opened the door slowly and poked my head into the hall. It was pretty much the way it was first time I was there. Deserted.

I jumped out, called into the shaft, "Lower away!"

The dumbwaiter creaked down. I stayed where I was, my eyes fixed on the door to Mrs. Wolch's apartment, wishing the rest of them would get up fast.

They came one at a time. For Albert Porter, being big, it was a tight fit. But he made it too.

"Okay, Howie, now where?" Denny whispered when he climbed out of the dumbwaiter.

"This way," I said, and headed toward Mrs. Wolch's door. We just stood there, too nervous to do anything. I was cracking my knuckles.

"Howie," my sister said, "use your knuckles on the door."

I gave her a dirty look, but all the same I reached up and rapped the door.

Which was just about the time that Denny said, "Hey, Howie, the petition. Better have it ready."

I reached into my pocket. It wasn't there.

39

HEART POUNDING, I searched my pockets like I was digging for gold. But see, the petition was gone. It must have fallen out when we were running down the street.

And natch, next second the door opened and a lady was standing there who I just knew had to be Mrs. Wolch.

I had never seen her before—I had been out in the hallway when she was talking, right?—so I didn't know what to expect. She wasn't very tall, and she was thin, with curly hair on the top of her head. Her eyeglasses were pushed up to her forehead. Her face was what you might call narrow, with this long nose. Actually she sort of looked like a poodle.

For a moment she just stood there, blinking at us. "Yes?" she finally said.

Denny, in his high voice, said, "You Mrs. Wolch?"

"Yes. Is this a scrap collection?"

Gloria, in a very loud voice, said, "My brother Howie has something important to tell you."

Everyone looked at me.

So did Mrs. Wolch. "Yes?" she said.

I heard myself saying, "We're . . . from P.S. 8."

"Yes?" Mrs Wolch said again as if it was the only word she knew.

What with my heavy breathing and all, I was finding it hard to say anything. But I finally said, "And . . . and . . . we need to talk to you about Miss Gossim."

"Miss Gossim?" Mrs. Wolch said. She was like an echo machine.

"Five-B," Billy Wiggins explained.

"On the second floor," Toby Robinson put in.

"I'm afraid I don't understand any of this," Mrs. Wolch said.

"It's Miss Gossim," I almost yelled with frustration. "She's getting fired. And you said Dr. Lomister could do it."

Mrs. Wolch's eyes got some light. "Ah!" she said. "I think I understand now. You're here to talk about the teacher who has been let go. The Robert Fulton School. Where Dr. Lomister is the principal."

"That's it," Gladys Halflinger said.

"So now you've all come to tell me something."

"It was my idea," my sister said.

Mrs. Wolch gave us another puzzled look. "But how did you all get here? I didn't hear my doorbell ring."

"We took the dumbwaiter," Gloria announced.

Denny said, "It's like a field trip."

"But—"

I couldn't stand it anymore. I suddenly burst out, saying, "Mrs. Wolch, we need to talk to you about Miss Gossim."

"Well, please, do so."

"See, she's being fired only because she's going to have a baby," I said.

"A baby?"

"Right. I mean, don't most people have to be born sometime in their life? And it's supposed to be majority rules. Look at the whole world war. All these people dying. And all she's doing is making one. You know, a replacement. And if you read the headlines, we need replacements. So we don't see why she has to be punished for that. And she needs her job. And her husband—his name is Smitty—is in the air force. Fighting in the war. With a P-38. And, anyway, it's not her fault she don't know where he is. It's the censors. Loose lips sink ships. Besides, she's the best teacher. So the thing is, it's not fair, and what's the whole war for anyway? And also, we had a petition which the whole class signed. Only I lost it. The whole thing is, we don't want her fired."

Mrs. Wolch, not saying anything at first, just stared at us. Then she said, "You had best come inside and we can talk about this."

40

WE WALKED INTO the apartment. It was like nothing I'd ever seen before. I mean *big*. Which for me meant the lady was well-heeled.

The place had a high ceiling, with a rug and a marble fireplace, plus curtains. All the furniture I saw was dark wood. Not one crack in any wall I saw. But the one thing I saw, more than anything else, is that she had a star flag hanging on her wall.

Anyway, like I told you, we went in, and she got us to sit down—some on the rug—and we started telling her all about what a great teacher Miss Gossim was. A whole lot of that stuff. She asked us some questions too. Was Miss Gossim a nice person? How did she teach? What did we like about her? You can guess. We gave her tons of answers.

Then after a while, this Mrs. Wolch said, "I want to thank you for coming. I will surely think about what you've told me."

"Can Miss Gossim stay?" I asked.

"We shall have to see," Mrs. Wolch said. "There are rules. And regulations."

"Mrs. Wolch," my sister suddenly blurted out, "don't you know there's a war on?"

"I think I do," she said quietly. "I had a son. He was in the Philippines. Now, when you leave, please take the stairway. Not the dumbwaiter."

I looked toward her star flag on her wall. That's when I took in that it was a gold one. Her son had been killed.

41

A FEW MINUTES later we were all standing in front of Mrs. Wolch's house. No one said anything. I was feeling kind of empty. See, we did this big thing, and then . . . nothing.

"Think she'll let Miss Gossim stay?" I asked nobody in particular.

"Guess we'll have to just wait and see," Gladys Halflinger said. "We tried."

Denny agreed. "Better than not trying," he said.

As Gloria and I walked home, she said to me, "You going to tell Mom?"

"If you want to, you can," I said.

I'm pretty sure she didn't. Least my mom never said anything to me.

Only thing I know is, that night I had the worst dreams of my whole entire life. It wasn't just pieces of my pop floating around, but some of Miss Gossim's body parts too.

I must have cried out.

"Howie," my sister said. "What's the matter?"

"Had a nightmare."

"Think of cake."

"What kind of cake?"

"Chocolate."

"How many layers?"

"Four."

"What's between the layers?"

"More chocolate."

"Anything else?"

"A cherry on top."

"That's the same cake I gave you."

"With all these shortages, I'm willing to share."

Cargo Ship Fights U-boat
to Finish.
52 of Crew Are Rescued.

U.S. Fliers Raid Pacific
Island Base.
New Anti-Tank Gun Revealed
by Army.

Royal Air Force Bombs
Berlin Again.

42

ON SUNDAY WE didn't do much of anything. My mom slept late. We read the funny papers. We listened to the radio. And you know what I did? I studied math. All day. It was boring, but I did it. See, I really wanted to give Miss Gossim that hundred percent as a going-away present.

And all the time I was thinking about my pop too. Where was he? Was he safe?

Americans Sweep Forward
in North Africa.

Churchill Pledges Invasion
of Europe Within Nine Months!

1,000,000 Nazi Children Urged
to Do War Work.

U.S. Repels Flotilla
in Aleutians.

43

MISS GOSSIM'S last day.

On the way to school I met Denny in front of his family's store.

"What do you think is going to happen?" he said.

"I dunno," I admitted.

We walked on some more and stopped to read the headlines.

Mr. Teophilo greeted us with a big smile. "Hey, how you doing, Denny? How you doing, Howie? Things are looking good. You hear from your fathers lately?" he asked.

"Which one?" I answered. "Me or Denny's?"

He laughed. "You can take your pick."

"My pop's on his way home," I said.

"I should be hearing from my dad soon" was Denny's answer.

"That's good. That's very good. Glad to hear it. And some more good news. The Dodgers won." He rubbed his gold chain.

We said, "So long," and kept going.

"You study for your math test?" I said.

"Yeah. You?"

"A lot."

"How come?"

"Felt like it."

Neither of us talked much, 'cause what was on our minds was Miss Gossim. In fact, we walked so slow that when we got to school the first bell just rang. Right away we had to line up. Then the second bell rang and we marched into class.

When we got to our room, Miss Gossim was there. She was looking pretty much the way she always did. The classroom was the same too, all neat. There was a new flower on her desk. A yellow daffodil with an orange middle. The date on the board was up, along with a list of class monitors. Also, what we were doing that day, with "Math test" being number one. What it didn't say was "Miss Gossim's last day."

Everybody was more quiet than usual. I figured the whole class knew what was going to happen. And what we had done. They were just watching Miss Gossim. Waiting. And, of course, though Miss Gossim was trying to act the way she usually did, you could tell it wasn't the same. I was also wondering if she knew what we did.

She took attendance. We pledged the allegiance. Got ink.

Then all of sudden the room sort of froze. Like a switch had been turned on. No one saying anything. No moving or hardly breathing. Nothing. All we could do was look at Miss Gossim. She looked back at us. We all knew what was happening. Except nobody wanted to say nothing.

It was Miss Gossim who finally said, "Let's just try to make it a good day."

Then she cleared her throat and said, "Pens out, please. Time for the math test."

The class did what she told us to do. Still, it didn't feel right.

"All right, class," Miss Gossim began, "let's do some quick times tables." And wouldn't you know, she picked the twelves. For me, that was like taking a walk in a tub of taffy.

She was just saying, "What is twelve times eight?"— which was a fatal pill—when the classroom door opened.

In came Lomister. Right behind him was Mrs. Wolch.

The class sat up, wondering what was going on.

Miss Gossim looked very nervous, though she tried to smile. "Good morning, Dr. Lomister, Mrs. Wolch," she said.

Then she turned to us. "Class," she said, "Mrs. Wolch is the acting superintendent of Brooklyn public schools. Please stand and say good morning to Dr. Lomister and Mrs. Wolch."

We stumbled up to our feet and said, "Good morning, Dr. Lomister. Good morning, Mrs. Wolch," in that sad singsong we always did.

Mrs. Wolch came to the front of the room. She put her hands together. Looked at us. Was that room quiet? I'm telling you, if some kid had a head louse, and that louse burped, you would have heard it.

"I wanted to tell you," she began, "that after a great deal of consideration—including a surprise visit from some of your classmates on Saturday—that the school district has decided to allow Miss Gossim to stay on for the rest of the year."

I swear, the whole class began to cheer. I mean, loud.

As for me, what I felt was relieved, and crazy happy. It was as if we had just won the war.

And Miss Gossim was smiling, and laughing, and

pushing her tears away, and a whole lot of other junk too. And then Dr. Lomister said something. But it was pretty stupid, and everybody knew it was stupid, not that anyone said it was stupid. See, stupid guys like that, you have to let them talk stupid. You just don't have to listen to stupid.

Then Miss Gossim said something to them. Only it was private, so I didn't hear. Then they went out.

It was then that she turned around and just stood there, looking at us. She was trying to talk, smile, not cry.

But she couldn't do much of anything. Not really. Instead, all she did was hold out her arms. And you bet, the whole class ran up to her and gave her this huge hug, and each other too, all at the same time.

Closest I've ever been to heaven in a school.

Except all of a sudden the door opened again. This time it was Mrs. Partridge. She didn't seem too happy.

We all got quiet. And looked at her.

"Denny Coleman," Mrs. Partridge said. "Your mother just called. You need to go right home."

See, the telegram from the government had come. Denny's father got killed.

44

ON THE WAY home I stopped to read the headlines at Mr. Teophilo's newsstand.

The old man lifted his face, eyes shut as always. "Hey, Howie," he called out. "How you doing, Howie? Hey, where's Denny?"

"Mr. Teophilo . . . his father got killed."

How can a man with shut eyes seem to close his eyes? But that's what it looked like. Then he shook his head from side to side and began to pull at his droopy mustache. "Oh, man, that's awful," he said. "That's terrible. I'm so sorry to hear that. I really am. You have to tell him how sorry I am."

"I will," I sort of said.

Those blind eyes of his, they began to tear. And he didn't wipe them away or nothing. Just let them come.

I stared at him.

"Now look here," he said, "you got to tell your friend Denny that Teo is feeling bad."

"I will," I said again, and started to go off.

"Hey, Howie!" Mr. Teophilo called. "Come here."

I went back.

He was holding out his hand. In his palm was his gold neck chain. "Here," he said dangling it before me. "I want you to give him this. Can you do that?"

"Sure."

"Tell him it's from Teo," he said, with a wipe of the back of his hand against his face. "Because Teo is sorry."

45

I GOT HOME, climbed the steps, walked into the apartment, and heard my sister talking to someone in the kitchen.

The door shut behind me.

"Hey, Howie, how you doing?" It was my pop.

I couldn't believe it. He was home. All this happening on the same day. I mean, Pop looked awful, but he was alive. He gave me a hug, finished a bowl of coffee, chomped down an apple, and went to sleep in his bed.

When my mom came in and we told her he was home, she was happy like I hadn't seen for a long time. She went to the door of their bedroom and just stared at him sleeping.

He opened his eyes and grinned at her. She went over and, for the first time in a long time, she kissed him, not his picture.

Later the three of us, every once in a while, we went in and kept looking at him in bed, asleep, but, see, alive.

He was home for three days. For most of the time he slept.

But that first night I told my mother about Denny's father.

"Poor Denny," she said, shaking her head. "And Mrs. Coleman. . . . It's so hard. . . ."

"Should I go over to see him?" I asked her. I was thinking I should. I wanted to give him Mr. Teophilo's neck chain anyway.

"Yeah. You should. He's your best friend."

"Should I tell him about Pop coming home?" I asked. She thought. "What do you think?"

"Mom, I feel bad Pop came home when . . . his didn't."

"Then keep that part to yourself for a while."

I went over to the Colemans' house. I could tell you

what it looked like, but it didn't matter. Just that mobs of people were there.

Denny was sitting next to his mother. He looked so pale. And sad.

I went up to him. "Mr. Teophilo said to give you this," I told him, and handed him the chain. "Said he's feeling bad too."

He took the chain, looked at it, bunched it up, and held it tight in his fist.

"You hear from your dad?" he said to me.

I swallowed hard.

He gazed at me from behind his specs, reached up, and pulled his earlobe.

I said, "He made it."

"That's good," he said.

"Yeah," I said.

And would you believe it, that night all I did was think about Denny and his dead dad. Not my own live one. How can you feel bad about feeling good?

46

ABOUT TWO WEEKS later there was this service for Mr. Coleman. I went, dressed in a suit I borrowed from some cousin two years older than me. Made me look like a baby hippo.

There was a coffin. It was covered with an American flag. Standing next to it was Denny with his mother.

Tons of people were there. There was all this talk about Mr. Coleman. Seemed like people just got up and said things. I kept wishing that people would say something about Denny.

I wanted to. But I was too scared.

But then, at one point, I looked at him, and he looked at me. When our eyes met, he pointed to his neck. I caught sight of the gold chain. Then he pulled his right earlobe.

I did the same.

Funny. That's all we did. But I knew him and me were all right.

Miss Gossim was there. I didn't speak to her. Afraid to. But later I saw she gave Denny a hug. I got these feelings of jealousy which made me feel like a low-down crawly worm.

Still, we stayed friends. Not that he ever smiled. Just sad. Always sad.

Which made me feel I had to do something for Denny. Something that would make him feel good. But I didn't know what.

47

PRETTY SOON IT was June and the last school day of the year. At three o'clock, right before the kids went out, Miss Gossim asked me to stay after class for a minute.

So I did, staying nervous in my seat, cracking my knuckles, wondering what I did wrong. Then she called me up, and I stood by her desk. She was really big with her . . . expecting. She had actually let us feel it, so we knew the baby was alive.

"Howie," she said to me, "I never wanted to talk about it before, but they—Dr. Lomister and Mrs. Wolch—told me what you did. That you—in your way—did help me."

"Wasn't just me," I said.

She smiled that great smile she had. "I'm sure that's so. But I'll always think it was you."

Then she said, "Howie, I'm going to miss you."

My heart upped and stopped. "Ain't you coming back to P.S. 8?" I asked.

"Aren't," she corrected. Then she said, "I don't know yet. We'll have to see, won't we? But, Howie, now that I'm leaving, I want you to know . . . you have been my favorite."

Her *favorite*! My big moment! But what did I do? I just stood there and mumbled, "Oh." Got red in the face.

"Have . . . you heard from Smitty?" I asked.

"Not yet," she answered.

Then all of a sudden she gave me this big hug, holding me against her belly. And wouldn't you know, that kid of hers, he wasn't even born yet, but he gave me a kick. After all I done for his mom! A kick, for cheese sake! And then, before I could say anything, Miss Gossim shooed me away.

48

LIKE ALWAYS, Denny was waiting for me.

"How come she asked you to stay?" he asked. He sounded almost angry.

"Just to say good-bye," I said.

"She say anything else?"

I looked at him. In his white shirt, bow tie, suspenders. Black hair slicked back. Frame glasses. Sad. "She said I should study math more. Get good grades. And you know what she said?"

"No."

"She said I should try to be more like my best friend— you."

"She really said that?" he asked with the first grin I'd seen from him in months.

"Cross my heart and hope to die."

"Swear," he said, and held out his hand, pinky out.

I hooked. "No fins."

"No fins."

We linked, chopped. Denny was standing a little taller.

We walked home, checked the newspapers at old Mr. Teophilo's. "Hey, Howie. Hey, Denny. Things are looking good. Except, wouldn't you know, the Dodgers lost again."

There was another gold chain around his neck.

49

ALL THAT SUMMER of 1943 I wondered about Miss Gossim. I couldn't believe she wouldn't come back. So, first day of new term in September and me in sixth grade, I went looking for her. Guess what? She wasn't there. Gone. And no one—not even Mrs. Partridge—knew what happened to her.

It wasn't the way things were supposed to happen. I mean, it should be that grown-ups stay put. It's kids that are supposed to go. But during the war, see, it was just the opposite. It was us kids who had the job of trying to keep things normal. Know what I'm saying? Denny stayed. His dad went away. I stayed. My pop kept going off.

And Miss Gossim went for good.

Germans Capitulate on
All Fronts.
Surrender Is Unconditional.

THE WAR IN EUROPE IS ENDED!

TUESDAY, AUGUST 8, 1945

**First Atomic Bomb Dropped
on Japan.
Missile Is Equal to
20,000 Tons of TNT.**

THURSDAY, AUGUST 10, 1945

Atom Bomb Loosed on Nagasaki.

TUESDAY, AUGUST 15, 1945

JAPAN SURRENDERS, END OF WAR!

50

THE WAR WAS over. On Hicks Street people were actually dancing. We took off our dog tags and flung them away.

Then the adults took back the job of keeping things normal.

But not quite. We moved from Brooklyn to Long Island, out to this place called Levittown, with a house of our own. Small maybe, but it seemed huge. And no cockroaches.

Pop got a job with the post office. "Keeps my feet on the ground," he used to say. But the funny thing was, at night, after he made his rounds, he started soaking his feet in, guess what? Salt water.

Same time, my mother quit work, but she got bored. Went back to school. Became a dental assistant. "Beats rivets," she'd say.

My sister? She grew up. We even got to be friends, sort of.

As for Denny Coleman, after we moved, I didn't see him no more. Once I sent him a picture postcard. It was of the Amagansett beach where those Nazi spies landed. He didn't answer.

His mother kept the store where it was. I know, because I went back once and looked. I think she got remarried. The store was there. Denny wasn't.

See, what I'm saying is, we moved away. My whole life got new. Changed.

Except for one thing.

51

I MAY BE OLDER—almost sixteen now—but when the nights get dark and I'm lonely or down in the dumps because the day is as hollow as the hole in a stale doughnut, do you know what I do? I think of Miss Gossim. Cross my heart and hope to die. I do. And if I think hard enough—and it's the night—all of a sudden there she is! Miss Gossim herself, sweet as ever, smelling like a Brooklyn Botanic field-trip flower. Like she was in that apartment of hers way back when the stars were in the sky and I visited her.

Next thing, I'm looking right up into those soft blue-gray eyes of hers and I'm saying, "Good-night, Rolanda Gossim."

Then she whispers, "Good-night, Howie Crispers."

But then, as if she was in some kind of movie, she starts to fade.

So in my head, I shout, "Hey, Miss Gossim, wait a minute! You can't go. I gotta find out. What happened to you? What's with Smitty? Where's your kid? Are you still a teacher?"

"Now, Howie," she says over her shoulder with a toss of that frilly blond hair, "don't you think it's time you forgot all that?"

"No," I say, "I can't. Besides, why should I?"

And in her most teacherlike voice, she answers, "Howie, don't you know? The war is over."

And she's gone.

And look at me—I'm sixteen, for cheese sake!—and it still makes me want to cry.

Know what I'm saying?

Use the following questions and activities to get more out of the experience of reading *Don't You Know There's a War On?* by Avi.

1. Why are there flags with blue stars hanging in the windows? What do gold stars mean?

2. Why does Howie follow Principal Lomister into the brownstone?

3. What secret signal do Howie and Denny have? What does it mean?

4. Principal Lomister is going to fire Miss Gossim. What does Howie think, at first, is the reason why? What is the real reason why?

5. How much time elapses from the beginning of the novel to the end? What device does Avi use to let you know this?

6. Explain why Howie is so concerned about failing his math test. How would the story change if he failed?

7. How does Howie feel about Miss Gossim? Use evidence to support your answer.

8. In what ways does Gloria contribute to helping Miss Gossim, both indirectly and directly?

9. Why do you think Miss Gossim reveals her secret to Howie? What circumstances might have influenced her that night?

Note: These literature circle questions are keyed to Bloom's Taxonomy: Knowledge: 1–3; Comprehension: 4–5; Application: 6–8; Analysis: 9–10; Synthesis: 11; Evaluation: 12–14.

10. When Howie's family gets a letter from his father, Howie refers to it as a "Swiss-cheese letter." How does Howie "Swiss-cheese" his own stories for different people in the book? Pick two examples and explain his motives for "Swiss-cheesing" the truth.

11. Why do you think Howie and Denny fell out of touch? If both their fathers had come home, how would the story be different?

12. The phrase "Don't you know there's a war on?" is used throughout the book as an answer or a reason for a variety of different situations and questions. List three different ways the phrase is used and how it applies to each situation.

13. In Chapter 29, Howie asks, "Don't grown-ups need kids— sometimes?" Do you think they do? Find examples of how kids help adults or take on adult responsibilities.

14. Howie and other characters in the story are constantly swearing to keep secrets and then breaking their promises. Do you think Howie is right to share his secrets? Why or why not? How would the story be different if the characters always kept their secrets?

Activities

1. In Chapter 21, Howie describes a war poster advertising "Buy War Bonds for Bombs!" Create your own poster promoting one of the wartime activities (such as gathering scrap) or containing a wartime warning, like "Loose Lips Sink Ships."

2. At the end of the book, Howie wonders what happened to Miss Gossim since he last saw her. Write a letter from Miss Gossim to Howie that answers his questions.

3. Choose a headline in the book, find out what it means, and research the events that occurred and the news that was being reported on that day in history.